EAST

The Conspiracy Starts

ANDREW D THOMPSON

Published by c9c LLC

East-20140901-1200

This book is dedicated to my parents, David and Shirley.
"Look ... I finished something!"

I would like to thank the following people:

My wife, Pam, for her unconditional and unfailing support
throughout this process

Jill, a friend since high-school, for her editing expertise

Debra, a colleague, for being my first reader

PROLOGUE

2005, May
Hong Kong International Airport

The man and the girl were the only two people not moving on the rail station at Hong Kong airport. They stood silently and waited.

The man was not old, but old enough to be the girl's father. At fourteen, she was slim with long black hair. Her Korean features contrasted with the Chinese face of her companion.

Without looking at the girl, he spoke in Korean. "Do you know what you need to do?"

She knew. "Identify the target. When he boards the train, I get in to the same compartment. When he gets off, I follow. When he meets someone, I photograph them. When they leave, I return to the hotel and wait."

"Excellent. We've been playing this game for a long time now --"

"Is it really a game?" she asked, looking up at him.

"Sometimes. But today is not a game, so be very careful."

She looked away again and nodded. "I understand."

His thoughts wandered away from the mission for a moment and he accepted the fact that this was the last time they would do this, or anything, together.

"Uncle ... " her voice brought him back to the mission.

"Yes?"

"I have to leave tomorrow. Can we go somewhere nice for dinner tonight?"

He smiled. "Of course! We have a lot to talk about before you leave."

***

The man saw the target as he entered the station and tapped the girl on her arm. "Over there, to the right. Yellow ball cap, blue bag. Do you see him?"

She looked at the people moving past them and saw the yellow cap. "I see him."

"Go. Good luck."

The girl started to work her way through the crowd and took up position behind the target. She followed as he entered the train and watched him sit down. She selected a seat a few rows behind him, on the same side of the train, and pulled a magazine from her bag. As she had been trained, she had already started to pay careful attention to the target as she couldn't afford to rely on the yellow hat as the only way to identify him. He might change it or throw it away in an attempt to alter his appearance. Much better to notice how he walked, what his shoes looked like, and try to get a good look at his face.

The train pulled out of the station on its way to the city and the girl watched out of the window at the trees and roads below them.

Although some of the other passengers were trying to sleep, the target was awake, but he didn't move or look around. The girl knew enough to be wary of people that didn't seem to be paying attention. Sometimes they weren't, but on the other hand she had been taught that they might be a skilled operator. Which category this target fell in to remained to be seen.

About ten minutes later they pulled in to Tsing Yi, half way to the expected destination. The target stayed in his seat and soon the train began moving again. The information had been that he would get off at Kowloon, but you could never be sure.

Another ten minutes and the train started to slow for Kowloon station. More people stood this time, including the target. The girl was already moving, away from the target, preparing to exit from a different door. He was still wearing the yellow cap, perhaps he was inexperienced? And then the yellow disappeared from sight, but not quickly enough to cause her any problems and she maintained her trailing position, varying from his left to right as they went.

As they exited the stairs from the station the target stopped. The girl kept moving and walked straight past him. She stopped before she got to the road side and look around as though disoriented. He was moving again, walking slowly to the north up Nathan Road. The girl didn't follow immediately. There were less people in that direction and his pace was slower than everyone else. To follow him at the same pace would give her away, especially if he had an accomplice. She looked around and not seeing any likely candidates, she started after the target.

He didn't stay on Nathan Road for long. A few hundred meters north was a bus stop and to the left an entrance in to Kowloon Park. She knew that if it had been Sunday, the park would be packed, but any other day she should have no trouble keeping him in sight.

She was a hundred meters behind him as she climbed the steps. She reached in to her bag for a small tourist camera and a hat. As she reached the top of the stairs. she spotted him walking straight ahead toward the sculpture area. She slowed and played with her camera before leaving the narrow path. She glanced through the trees. The sculpture walk was a wide paved area, sculptures lined up in two straight lines. She could see an alcove on the other side containing several benches. One of the benches was occupied by a man with an identical blue bag. He was reading a newspaper, which hid his face from sight. She turned the camera on. The target was walking toward the man on the seat. He sat next to him and placed the bag on the ground, next to the other.

The girl looked around to see if anyone else was interested in this pair, but nobody seemed to care what they were doing. A few people were looking at the exhibits and one person was taking photographs. She felt like she was going to be able to blend in to the scene.

She headed toward a sculpture and inspected it. Some children ran past. Raising the camera she started to photograph the sculpture. She wasn't sure what it was supposed to be, but somebody must like it. As she moved around the object, the men moved in to the picture. She changed the zoom and took several shots. The newspaper was lowered and she got a good shot of the faces of both men. The men exchanged a few words and the target stood, taking the other bag with him and exited to the north. She watched him go from the corner of one eye, but otherwise ignored him.

The other man folded his newspaper, stood, picked up the bag and walked to the south. He walked toward the girl, who moved on to the next sculpture. He went past, glancing quickly at her but without pausing, which was fine with her.

She was left alone, an occasional person passing by, as though nothing had happened.

Mission accomplished. Almost. Now she had to get back to the hotel without a tail.

She waited ten minutes, feigning interest in the other objects, then retraced her steps out of the park, crossed Nathan Road and went in to a burger restaurant. As she stood in line she surveyed the people who followed her in, recalling the people she had passed. After a couple of minutes she was satisfied that if anyone had followed they were still outside.

The girl ordered a drink and took it over to a vacant table near the window where she repeated her people watching. Nobody seemed to be loitering, no oddly parked cars, and nobody that she recognized. She waited ten minutes, then left the restaurant. Outside she fiddled with the straw, and finished the last of the drink. She tossed the container in to the trash and walked east on Humphreys Avenue, away from the park. This was a narrow street with access for pedestrians on one side only. She made use of the shop windows to monitor people behind her. She paused a couple of times to window shop and doubled back toward Nathan Road and the park. Nobody changed direction. She doubled back again, continuing away from the park.

At the first opportunity she turned north and then one block later, west toward Nathan Road. As she did so, she took off the hat and placed it back in her bag on top of the camera.

Ten minutes later she reached the hotel and satisfied that no one had followed, she entered. At the elevator she rode up to the ninth floor and walked down two floors.

In her room, she lay on the bed to wait for her uncle to return.

***

Her uncle had stood behind some trees and watched the girl as she photographed the men. He hadn't wanted to use her, especially on her last trip to see him, but the target would have recognized him instantly. He was left with no choice, but he watched her with pride. She was doing well.

He saw the target leave to the north and the other man take his bag and walk south.

He didn't care about the second man, his only concern was for the target. Actually, that wasn't true, he realized. He was also concerned about the time. This was his last day with the girl and time was precious. He decided that he would finish it here, in the park. There was a good chance that the target's next stop would be Macau, where he could spend and launder some of the money that he had probably just picked up. Which meant leaving the park to the west and the nearest ferry.

He moved ahead to intercept the target at the lake. A few minutes later he was standing on the bridge over the bird lake listening to two hundred birds. The target passed the other end of the bridge on his way to the exit and he hurried after him. As they left the lake behind them they could both see the bridge ahead, which led over Canton Road to the waterfront and the ferry to Macau.

A block of public restrooms was on the left. No one was

around. He closed on the target and wrapping his arm around his throat jerked him to the side of the path and forced him behind the building. His victim was struggling, not sure what was happening until he felt a foot behind his knees and fell to his knees on the ground. The arm released his throat and while he was massaging it, the last thing he felt was something heavy on the back of his head.

The man pulled on a pair of surgical gloves and dragged the target to a tree where he sat him against the trunk. A roll of utility tape from his bag helped secure the lifeless wrists together behind the tree. One more piece under his chin and tied behind the tree held him up.

While he waited for the target to wake, he reached for the blue bag and opened it. He raised his eyebrows. As expected, it was cash. He didn't bother to count it, the amount was irrelevant.

He went though the target's pockets and found a wallet, which he emptied. The contents went in to his own bag.

To help the target wake up, he pushed the wallet in to the mouth and used another length of tape around the head to hold it in place. Then he gently slapped the face until the head started to move.

Gradually the target regained consciousness, only to discover that it wasn't a dream. It would have been bad enough to be in this situation and being robbed, but when he saw the man standing over him, the blood left his face. This was the end and he knew it.

The man spoke to him. "As you can see, I have your money. I have not counted it because I don't care how much or little it took for you to betray our department. And as you can tell from the tape around your mouth, I don't want to hear what you have to say. So just listen. We knew what you were doing, because you weren't very good at it. The information that you just sold was fabricated for this occasion. Worthless. Well, not entirely. They may spend some time and resources trying to take action against it, but it won't matter to us. Thank you anyway."

He saw the terrified look in the target's eyes, but it had no effect on him.

Taking a knife with a six inch blade from his bag, he placed the tip against the man's chest over his heart. The target began to whimper. Without a word he quickly pushed the knife in until the blade completely disappeared.

The targets eyes rolled back in his head and the head fell to one side. He withdrew the blade.

The cash was transferred to his own bag and a minute later he checked the target for a pulse, which he did not find. He removed the tape and wallet from his victim, who he left lying on the ground.

He mentally made a note to fill the new vacancy in the Bangkok office.

The tape, gloves, and knife went in to a small bag, which he sealed.

Packing everything over his shoulder, he took a last look around for anything he might have left. As he didn't see anything, he discretely rejoined the path and headed back to the hotel. He was looking forward to the rest of the day with the girl.

***

Later that afternoon, the man and the girl were sitting in a private area at a nice restaurant. The food had been good. They had dressed up for the occasion and he thought how pretty she was. He smiled as he remembered that he thought that every day.

"Have you enjoyed your trip?" he asked.

"Of course, I always do. Thank you for everything!"

"I'm sorry to have to say this ..." he said, pausing to make sure that he used the right words, "but this is going to be the last trip."

She was puzzled. "Forever?"

"Yes. My job is dangerous and there are things which I can not explain to you, but it will not be safe for you to be associated with me now that you are getting older." He saw the look of disappointment in her face. "Also, your grandmother contacted me. She is not well and asked that you stay with her in Korea in case she needs you."

"This isn't fair!"

"Life is not fair," he said sternly. He softened his voice. "After your parents died and you went to live with your mother's mother ... how has it been?"

"Everyone is leaving me. I never knew my parents and now grandmother is sick. You are the only family left in my life. Why are *you* leaving me?"

He thought he saw her eyes beginning to moisten and he moved to sit next to her.

"If we could stay together, I would. But it just isn't possible," he said. "You've been visiting for nine years now, since you were five. I've tried to teach you things that will help you in life, because the world is a dangerous place. I want you to keep practicing your Tae Kwan-Do. Please?" He took her hand and looked in to her eyes. "Promise me that you will stay strong. Healthy and strong."

She promised.

They sat in silence for a while.

"You've never asked much about your parents, do you have any questions for me?" he asked.

She thought for a moment. "You knew my father, yes?"

"I knew him very well. He loved your mother and you too, even though he never saw you."

"Is he dead?"

"We think so, but we don't know for sure. As you know, he just disappeared one day, about a month before you were born."

"He didn't run away?" she asked.

Her uncle scoffed at the idea. "No. Not him. He would never have left the two of you unless there was a very good reason."

"Did you know my mother well?"

"I met her a few times. She was pretty, like you, and very kind. But she was strong when she had to be. She was a lot like you."

"My grandmother never talks about my parents. Didn't she like my father?"

He smiled. "I think she believed that your mother could have done better. But perhaps all mothers think that way."

The girl straightened as a question came to her. "Was my father Korean?"

Her uncle paused. "You know I am not family. I am your uncle because I wanted to help look after you in some small way." He paused. "Why do you ask?"

She shrugged. "The way that grandmother talks about foreigners made me think that this could be why she didn't like my father."

"You're very perceptive. He was Chinese."

The girl nodded.

"But love is love," he added, "and love has very few boundaries."

"What is your job?"

"Ah, you've asked that one before. The answer is the same. I work for the government and I fix problems."

A silence settled over them again. The private room was very quiet, with only an occasional sound of plates or glassware from beyond the door. But there was nothing awkward about this silence.

"Will I be able to contact you?"

"I'm going to be traveling a lot so I won't be easy to find. I'll send birthday cards. Ah ... I never mentioned it but I set up a bank account for you some years ago and I've been putting money in it. I intended it to help with your education, but you may use it any way that you want, once you are twenty."

She lowered her head. "Thank you, uncle."

"You're a good girl. Make your parents proud."

Her shoulders were moving as she tried to hold back her tears. He put both arms around her in a hug.

"Aigoo, aigoo. Everything will be all right. Just stay strong."

She quietly cried in to his shoulder for a while and he gently held her until she stopped, then she moved back and wiped her eyes.

"Let's go back to the hotel and pack," he said.

***

The girl sat in a large Business Class seat on the flight from Hong Kong to Seoul. She had cried a little more at the airport and if her eyes had not been so full of tears, she would have seen that her uncle was also close to tears himself.

He had given her an envelope just as she was being escorted on to the aircraft by an airline employee.

"Open this after you take-off," he had said and hugged her tightly.

She reached in her bag for the envelope and opened it. Inside was a generous amount of cash, a bank draft, two business cards, and a letter. She turned the cards over in her hand. One had her uncle's name on one side, but nothing else. The other was for a manager at the Seoul branch of a large international bank. The bank draft was for her grandmother. She unfolded the letter.

Sora,

Please give the draft to your grandmother. Your father would have wanted me to help look after you and this is the best I can do at the moment.

Go to the bank when you are twenty and show them the business card.

Keep my name close to your heart, where others can't see it. It is dangerous to both of us for you to try and contact me or use my name. Whatever stories you hear about me in the future, please look on me kindly.

We may not meet again and if we do it will be in the distant future.

Stay strong.

I will never forget you.

Your Uncle,

Jiang Bo

EAST

The Conspiracy Starts

CHAPTER ONE

Present Day | March 03 | 12:30
A Cat Cafe, Seoul, South Korea

Park YeJin sat at a corner table, her back to the wall, looking out on to the street two floors below. Occasionally she would lift her drink and take a sip, giving the impression of a woman without a care in the world. The cat sitting on the adjacent table had the same air. The location had been chosen to give her the upper hand and she intended to use it.

She was actually a little nervous, as anyone would be, meeting with an agent from their national security service.

There were a few other people in the cafe, sipping their drinks and playing with the cats. She would have liked to have a cat herself and she had the space, unlike a lot of other people in the city. But whilst the companionship would be nice, she wasn't ready for the responsibility of something or someone else relying on her. So, like the other customers, she came to a cat cafe to satisfy that desire.

When the man wearing a black suit entered the otherwise empty cafe she pretended not to notice, keeping her eyes on his reflection in the window. His discomfort was obvious even from across the room, his look of disgust giving away his lack of field experience. YeJin fought a smile and took another sip from her drink. He didn't seem to have changed since they had last met, still the same junior she had worked with at the National Intelligence Service. She hadn't been impressed then and didn't expect to be this time. In some ways it was almost an insult that he had been the one who was sent. Perhaps that was the intention?

He crossed to her table and sat down without a greeting or invitation. For someone who was her junior both in age and previously in the workplace, this was an insult, or at least very rude.

"Ryu DaeHo, before you sit down ..." She tapped her drink container.

"You want another drink?" he asked, confused.

"No, but you are supposed to buy one," she reminded him. "It's the rule."

He paused for a moment, then got up. He returned, uncomfortably, with a pink drink, the cheapest drink they had. He sat down again.

YeJin looked at the drink and couldn't hide her smile this time.

She needled him once more. "And don't forget to use the hand sanitizer before you touch the cats."

"I won't be touching the damned cats," he said irritably, "I'm allergic to them."

YeJin smiled sympathetically, as if she didn't know. "Really? Then perhaps you should get to the point. Why did you want to meet?"

He kept his eyes on a large cat which was getting closer and said, "We would like you to do some work for us."

"Work?"

"Yes, we need an identity packet created."

"We?"

"The NIS. Your old employers. Who else?"

"Why not produce it internally?"

"Everyone is just so busy and we need these in a hurry. We'd like you to work away from our office and we will arrange delivery of any materials you need. It will be international items.

A drivers license, passport, credit card. The usual." The cats were beginning to make his eyes water. "We thought you would appreciate the business and we're paying top dollar. How about it?"

"I'm flattered." She wasn't. "But I've retired." She was.

No response.

YeJin pointed to her camera. "I'm a photographer now."

No response.

"I don't do that any more."

No response.

"They fired me, remember?"

No response.

She tilted her head and raised her eye-brows. "Are you awake?"

He stood, still warily eying the large cat, and placed a business card on the table. He tapped the card twice. "I need you to confirm by tomorrow. Contact me at my new number."

She watched his back as he left, and grinned as he sneezed twice while exiting the cafe. It had definitely been a calculated insult on their part, but she felt a little better about it. Perhaps because she had never been a field agent, this had been a little exciting.

The large cat jumped on her lap. "Thank you," she said as she scratched his head, "we did well."

***

Rubbing his eyes, Ryu DaeHo left the cafe, paused for a break in the traffic, and crossed the street. When he had walked until he was out of sight of the building he pulled out his phone and dialed a number from memory. It was answered after two rings.

"*Will she do this job for us?*" No pleasantries, just straight to business.

"She hasn't agreed yet, but I'm confident that she will."

"*I hope that your confidence is not misplaced.*" The voice paused. "*I believe we were clear about our desire to have a positive outcome from this meeting?*"

"Yes, sir, and if necessary I have prepared a little pressure to help persuade her." He paused. "But she was fired in disgrace, why would we use someone with her record --?"

"*You do not need to understand, just make sure it happens.*" The voice was slightly raised, enough for him to regret what he had just asked.

"Yes, sir. I will have her confirmation by tomorrow."

The call ended abruptly. He had been dismissed. As he returned the phone to his pocket the sudden recollection of the meeting made him realize that YeJin had completely dominated him.

He felt like he had just attended his own interrogation.

CHAPTER TWO

Jung RaeWon had watched the NIS agent enter the cafe, verified that he was alone, and listened to the audio as Park YeJin skillfully used the felines to her advantage and caught the agent off-guard. And while it was true that they had not learned anything that they did not already know, they did now have some better idea of what was being asked of them.

When the NIS had contacted YeJin for a meeting she had immediately gone to RaeWon to get his advice.

It was now three years since they had both left the NIS, forced out after an operation had resulted in the death of an agent in the field. YeJin had been blamed because the failure was thought to have been caused by the documents that the agent was carrying; documents that she had created. The dead agent had been someone RaeWon had partnered with on several operations and considered a friend. But even through his grief, he had been able to see that YeJin was a scapegoat. She had been forced out and the NIS lost one of their best document people. It hadn't made much sense at the time to either of them, but it did bring them closer together which was something he did not regret. RaeWon had left a month later, partly out of loyalty to YeJin, but also because he was tired of seeing people with little or no field experience being promoted to positions where they could hurt people with their lack of knowledge. And the death of his friend had seemed strange at the time. Nothing he could put his finger on, but definitely strange.

They had kept a low profile since that time, YeJin starting a photography business and RaeWon becoming a freelancer in the corporate intelligence market. They had not attempted contact with anyone, even former friends, at the NIS and no one had made contact with them either.

Until now.

When people who have ruined your reputation come calling for help, you have to treat it as suspicious. But RaeWon treated everything with suspicion. This was what had made him such a good operative and certainly much better than this inexperienced junior from their past.

As Ryu DaeHo put the phone in his pocket and walked away, RaeWon lowered the camera and took out his own phone to send a message to YeJin:

Leave now. I will check for a tail.

A few minutes later she left the building and stood for a moment to make sure that even an inexperienced follower could not miss her. Then she walked away. RaeWon carefully scanned the vehicles and pedestrians for anyone taking an interest in her. There were a few; a good looking woman always attracts attention, but no one that concerned him.

A light rain began to fall.

***

An hour later RaeWon and YeJin were sitting across from each other in the small kitchen at YeJin's studio looking at video made in the cafe and listening to Ryu DaeHo's phone conversation about persuading her to do the job.

The recording ended.

"I'm worried," she said.

"You should be --"

"Well, thanks for being optimistic!" she said sarcastically.

He met her gaze. "If you're worried, you'll be ready for whatever stupid thing he has cooked up. And there are two of us. And each of us is twice as bright as he is. We'll be okay. I just wish they had left us alone."

"Do you really believe that they need me to do this work?"

RaeWon lifted his coffee. "No, I don't, and neither do you. The whole thing smells."

"Should I do it?"

"No." RaeWon put his coffee back on the table. "I think you want as much distance between you and this job as possible. It's just a feeling, but I think you should turn it down. Let's do that sooner rather than later and hope that they move on to someone else."

"I agree."

While YeJin dialed the number from the business card and enabled the speaker, RaeWon started the recorder. She straightened involuntarily as the call was answered.

"*Hello?*"

"This is Park YeJin --"

"*Yes. When should I deliver the materials?*"

"I'm sorry, but I'm not going to be able to do the job for you."

A brief pause. "*We'll double the fee.*"

YeJin was surprised and looked at RaeWon who shook his head. "No, I'm sorry," she said. "I'm out of the business."

"*YeJin, I'm sure you realize that we are not the kind of people you want as enemies. I strongly suggest that you reconsider.*"

"I don't want to do it. Please find someone else." She quickly disconnected the call and stared at the phone for a few seconds. "Sorry, I panicked for a moment. Why did he have to mention being enemies?"

RaeWon shrugged. "I don't know, it seemed a little extreme. Of all the people they could have sent, he would be my very last choice. His negotiation skills need a little help."

"Is that what you really think?"

He grinned. "I thought you wanted me to be optimistic?"

***

Ryu DaeHo moved the phone away from his face but didn't put it down. Instead, he held it in mid-air with a look of bewilderment on his face. Why had she turned down a very generous offer for something that she could have done in her sleep? All that money for a few hours work. Crazy!

Of his many faults, the biggest was that he was unable to see them. Any of them. Which is why he was unable to comprehend that he had approached YeJin in the wrong way. But, despite his shortcomings, he was still curious to know why they wanted to use someone who had been dismissed from the NIS because of poor performance. Like everyone else, he had heard the rumors: an error on a passport had caused the loss of an agent. Despite their bosses keeping quiet about the whole event, in the hope that people would forget and move on, it had developed in to a pervasive myth. Perhaps in part because of that other agent who had left at almost the same time. What was his name? Yes - Jung RaeWon, an agent with his own, stellar, reputation. But why were they so insistent on using Park YeJin? It made no sense, or none that he could imagine.

Oh well, orders were orders. If she was their choice then he would have to change her mind and he had a plan for that. He dialed a number.

"Hello? - - Yes, that project we discussed - - Uh huh - - Tonight. Call me when it is complete."

He hung up.

CHAPTER THREE

YeJin had spent the rest of the afternoon editing some photographs from a session a few days before. As she rubbed her eyes for the fifth time she decided that it might be a good idea to go home and when she looked at the clock, the time confirmed it. Some food on the way would be welcome too. Turning off the lights she headed for the door.

The rain was now coming down a little faster and a little harder. YeJin opened her umbrella, its bright color illuminated by the lights from the surrounding buildings in the dim light of the evening. Holding it over her head it failed to provide cover from the rain which came at her sideways. So, resigning herself to the fact that she was going to get wet, she tilted it into the rain to get a little more protection, and started walking toward the road to try and hail a taxi. Finding a taxi might be hard in this weather, she thought.

The weather matched her thoughts. Despite RaeWon's forced optimism about getting the NIS to move on and out of their lives again, she wasn't convinced.

She had gone about a hundred meters when she heard a voice behind her.

"Park YeJin-shi!"

She turned and saw two men coming toward her from the

shadows. At the same time she heard sounds between her and the main road. Twisting her head round she saw another two men moving to block her way out. Turning again, YeJin felt her arm grabbed and she was pulled to the side of the street as she dropped the umbrella.

***

Lee Sora tried to will herself deeper into her coat as she pulled the almost empty backpack higher on to her back. She was wet, cold, and could really use a hot drink. She had been working as a waitress at a small cafe, but the owner had let her go today. He was really sorry, he told her, but his wife's cousin had arrived in town and needed work so he had no choice. He paid her an extra two weeks money and continually told her how sorry he was. She believed him, but that wasn't going to help pay her bills. She was staying with an acquaintance temporarily but knew that she was going to have to find somewhere else very soon.

As she passed the entrance to a lane, she heard someone calling a name. She involuntarily glanced toward the sound and saw a woman with a bright umbrella facing away from her and two men walking toward her. The woman turned her head back and forth and was grabbed by another man, who pulled her to the edge of the lane against a pole. She watched the umbrella fall to the ground. There was no mistaking that this as a friendly encounter. One-on-one perhaps it could have been a quarrel between lovers, but three - no, four - against one? No way.

As the woman was held against the utility pole, the wires and cables radiating from it made the scene look as though she had been captured by a spider in its web.

Sora looked around for a policeman, but the streets were mostly deserted, of course. She took off her backpack and reached for the phone. No power. Why now of all times? The voices from the men were muffled by rain and she couldn't make out what they were saying. The woman obviously needed help and Sora didn't think twice. Slipping the backpack over one shoulder, she unzipped her coat and turned in to the lane and pretended to look at her phone as if preoccupied.

Two things could happen, she knew. One, they would see her and run. Or two, they wouldn't.

***

YeJin felt the rough pole through her jacket as she was pushed against it. Everything had happened so fast that she had not looked at their faces. She looked her assailant in the eyes defiantly but she didn't recognize him.

"Yes, take a good look, I'm not afraid of you," he said. "And listen well to my message."

A message? It must be from Ryu DaeHo. "You couldn't write me a letter?" she asked.

A short laugh. "He was right, you're a feisty one! Now pay attention. You will call Ryu DaeHo and accept the commission. You will call him tonight."

"And what if I don't?"

He pushed her harder against the pole making her wince. "Really? You don't have enough imagination to guess what we might be forced to do? You have many things that could be damaged or lost." He listed them slowly. "Your business. Friends. Family. Your arms. Legs. Your pretty face." He paused. "Your sight."

One of the gang saw a figure enter the lane and called out to it, "Go away. This way is closed." He moved towards the small person in the big coat and raised a hand as a sign to halt.

***

As Sora advanced up the lane, pretending to look at her phone, she continuously took in the situation which unfolded as she got nearer to the men. In her mind she channeled all the unhappiness of the day, no — the previous three months, ready for a confrontation. Three months ago she had been in a similar situation and the memory still lingered. Right now, it felt as if it had happened yesterday.

She continued forward, the phone in her left hand and a firm grasp on the backpack with her right.

One of the men had seen her. "Go away. This way is closed."

She saw his outstretched arm and headed toward him.

"Ahjussi! Can you help me?" she asked as she got nearer. It didn't look as though any of them were displaying any weapons. All their hands were visible, and empty.

"Leave, brat!"

Sora swung the backpack off her shoulder, got one of the straps looped over the outstretched arm, pulled him toward her, ducked under the arm to move behind him, and brought him to the ground with an elbow to the side of the head. He knelt there, clutching his head trying to see straight. Two of the men moved in, one angling behind her. She spun around and floored the second with a kick to the head. The man holding YeJin watched the events in disbelief. The remaining guy grabbed her from behind in both arms. She lifted her feet to become dead weight, her wet coat letting her slip to the ground. As he bent over she rammed her phone into the nearest eye and grabbed his ear, twisting hard. He screamed. The first man was back on his feet and angry. Sora dodged his kick and landed one of her own between his legs. As he bent over, her knee met his face.

The leader had pulled a knife. YeJin screamed when she saw it and scratched at his face. Alerted by the scream, Sora aimed a kick at his wrist and the knife clattered to the floor. He pushed YeJin hard to the ground and fled, holding his wrist. As he left he called back, "Call him! It will only get worse for you!"

A moment later, YeJin and Sora were alone. The rain continued to fall as though nothing had happened.

"Help me back to my studio, please." YeJin was a little stunned from where her head had hit the ground.

Sora bent to retrieve her backpack. "Of course. Where is it?" she asked.

"Just back here a little way. Help me up."

The two women slowly made their way back up the lane to where YeJin had left a few minutes before and were soon inside, the door locked behind them. They went in to the back area where Sora saw a small kitchen with a table and chairs, and a sofa. She helped YeJin to the sofa and hunted round in the kitchen to make an ice-pack for her head. First aid accomplished, Sora sat at the table.

"Can I call anyone?" she asked. Now that it was over she remembered the authorities. "We should call the police!"

YeJin shook her head and instantly regretted it. She reached in to her bag for a phone. "I'll call a friend. Do you mind staying until he gets here?"

"Of course. But what was going on back there? Did you know those guys?"

"When my friend gets here, I'll explain then." YeJin finished dialing and put the phone to her ear.

"Okay. Do you have any towels here. And a hot drink?" Sora asked hopefully, starting to shiver as the adrenalin wore off and she realized that a puddle was forming around her.

"Help yourself, just look around." The phone was answered. "RaeWon! I need you to come back to the studio. I was attacked as I left - - Yes, I'm going to be okay. Someone came along and helped - - Yes, she's okay too - - Yes, a girl. Look, just come over and I'll tell you everything - - Okay, hurry!"

Sora made them both some hot chocolate and handed a mug to YeJin, who sat with the ice clutched to her head and eyes closed. She draped a blanket around the shoulders of the woman on the couch and then started to explore. She had found a small towel in the kitchen, but needed something larger. She quickly found an empty storage room and a small bathroom with a shower. A couple of towels were on a shelf so she took one and started to dry her hair, taking the other to YeJin.

"Are you feeling better?" she asked.

"I am, thank you. And thank you for your help out there, I don't know what would have happened if you hadn't come along. You were very brave. Where did you learn to fight like that?"

***

Jung RaeWon quietly entered the building from the rear. He

heard their voices from the kitchen and hurried over. As he entered the room, he noticed a slim girl holding a towel in one hand and a mug in the other. She seemed very alert and it looked as though she was about to throw the drink at him. He bowed slightly in her direction and moved to YeJin.

"Are you okay? Who was it? What did they say?" he said as he took the ice-pack from her head. "Did they hurt you?"

"I'm okay. It was a message from Ryu DaeHo --"

"What did he say?" he asked.

"He said that if I don't take the contract that they will start destroying things in my life. He even said that my eyes were at risk."

Sora was starting to get alarmed. "What have I got involved in?" she asked.

Jung RaeWon thought about that for a moment. "It's a long story. I doubt they will remember your face and won't have any way to track you down. But ..." He considered how he would go about it in their position. "Do you work nearby?"

Sora shook her head. "Not anymore, I lost my job today."

"Where are you staying?"

"With a friend, but I need to change that arrangement too."

Jung RaeWon looked at YeJin, who raised her eyebrows. He knew the un-voiced question. "How about we explain all this to you tomorrow? Stay here for the night, out of sight, and we'll get together in the morning." He waited for Sora's response, but he couldn't read her thoughts at all.

"Go take a shower, you look like you're melting," urged YeJin.

Sora looked down at her wet cloths, looked back at RaeWon, nodded, and headed out of the room. He went back to inspecting YeJin's head and concluded that she would be fine. Suddenly, he walked over to Sora's backpack and started going through it.

YeJin looked confused. "What are you doing?" she hissed.

He didn't answer but when he stood up, he was holding a drivers license. He took out his phone and photographed the card, which he then replaced as efficiently as he had taken it.

"Aren't you the least curious about who she is and why she was there at exactly the right time? And with exactly the right skills?" he asked her. "Because I am."

"I'm grateful that she was there, they were scaring me!"

"I'm grateful too, but I'll just run a quick check." He grinned. "Just so that we know how grateful to be!"

***

Ryu DaeHo's phone rang. Good, he thought, another item to cross-off his to-do list.

"It went well?" he asked. Confident of the outcome, it was more of a statement than a question. Four men against one, untrained woman? No contest.

"*We gave her the message,*" said the voice. "*But someone interfered.*"

"Who? What happened?" He was feeling less confident now.

"*Someone came along and beat-up my men.*"

"Who was he? Anyone we know? Where they working together?"

"*It was a woman, not known to us, and I don't think there were together.*"

"Okay. I must be having trouble hearing you. A woman beat-up four trained, experienced men. Does that cover it?"

"*Yes, but we did give the message to the target.*"

"I understand, but it might not have had as much weight after you were all forced to leave!"

"*Look, asshole, perhaps your information was bad and you sent us in unprepared?*"

"You had better hope that she calls to accept!" He hung-up.

Chapter Four

March 04 | 07:00

They had stayed at the studio until Sora had dried-off and they had found some dry clothes for her. Sora had not minded being on her own in a strange place for the night. She saw the logic of being off the street and away from the thugs.

Jung RaeWon had offered to have both of the women stay at his apartment and had been surprised when YeJin had accepted. He knew this was more to do with how frightened she had been than his personal charms, but he was happy to feel that she was safe. As a gentleman he had given up his bed in favor of the couch and this morning YeJin had woken to the smell of fresh coffee.

RaeWon noticed her head as she poked it out of the bedroom and thought, not for the first time, that he would like to see that sight every morning.

"Good morning," she said sleepily, as she arranged her hair with one hand.

"Did you sleep well?" he asked.

"Yes, thank you. Did you run a check on my guardian angel?" She took the mug of coffee that he held out for her.

"I did --"

"And how grateful are you feeling toward her?" she said, poking fun at the fact that he was suspicious of everything and everyone.

"Well ... I have to say that I don't hate what I found out."

"Very generous of you, but what did you discover?"

"Lee Sora, age twenty-three, no criminal record, Black Belt in TKD and several wins in local tournaments. I couldn't find any trace of links to the NIS. I spoke on the phone with the owner of the cafe that she just left and he was glowing in his praise for her. I think he already regrets having to let her go. But his loss might be our gain."

"What do you mean?"

"I think I want to offer her a job."

"Really?" YeJin was surprised as RaeWon had always preferred working alone. "Why? And what would she do for you?"

"For us. I think we could share her." Secretly he wanted someone to help look out for YeJin but didn't want to tell her that he was worried. "I haven't found anyone reliable to help me and I have a hunch that she might be the one. It's hard to find people who are that level-headed in tough situations. And you can use someone part-time around the studio, yes? What do you think?"

YeJin thought about it as she cradled the mug in two hands. "Do you like her?" she said not looking at anything in particular.

RaeWon snorted. "What? No! I just have a good feeling about her. I think she will be useful."

YeJin continued cradling her coffee as she looked at him. "How can I get the NIS off my back?"

"Good question. They seem very determined that you, and only you, do the work. If we want to stay in Seoul, or anywhere in South Korea, without permanently looking over our shoulders --"

YeJin cut him off. "We? Are we getting married?" she teased him. "I appreciate your help but I don't want to drag you in to this mess."

"You already asked for my advice and help. I'm involved." He poured some more coffee. "I think you should consider doing the job." He saw the look of surprise on her face and watched as it was replaced with acceptance.

"I suppose you're right."

"But what really concerns me,' he continued, "is why they picked *you*. I know you have the skills, but they seem to be making a very clumsy approach. I wish we knew what their motive is. It makes me nervous."

"Me, too. But ... how much are you going to tell Sora? We can't let her get involved blindly."

"The question is, do we let her go and possibly be a target for the NIS? Or do we keep her close, where she might still be a target, but we can look out for her?" Jung RaeWon knew that both scenarios included some degree of risk. "We need to talk to her."

"Okay, why don't we take some breakfast over for her?"

***

Two hours later the three of them were, again, sitting around the table in what had been Sora's home for the night. Rather naturally, she had seemed a little shocked by the revelations of Jung RaeWon and Park YeJin's past employment.

Jung RaeWon looked over at Sora. "So that brings you up to speed. What do you think? Do you want to stay, or would you prefer to leave town for a while? If you stay, we can offer you some work and you're welcome to stay here. If you leave town, I can give you some money to help out."

As he looked at her, he thought that this must be a lot for her to take in and probably like nothing she had experienced before. He also realized he had no idea what she was thinking. Not a clue. He hoped that she would decide to stay.

Sora carefully considered everything for a moment and looked him straight in the eye. "What did the background check say about me?"

RaeWon took this in stride without displaying any emotion, but YeJin gasped, quickly putting her hand to her mouth.

"What makes you think I ran a check on you?" he asked neutrally.

"You went through my backpack and took my driver's license."

YeJin stifled another gasp and he made a mental note never to play on her team in a betting game. "It didn't say anything out of the ordinary. You've never been arrested and don't seem to have ties to the NIS." He leaned forward. "And we want you to know how much we appreciate what you did last night. If you're interested I'd like to offer you some work."

"What kind of work? Bodyguard?"

YeJin was curious. "Why a bodyguard?"

"I think he wants someone to watch over you."

YeJin punched him on the arm. "Is that right?"

He sensed he was losing control of the situation; not a familiar experience. Sora was someone that he shouldn't under-estimate.

"Partly. Look, Sora, you came out of nowhere at just the right time. We don't know why the NIS wants YeJin to do this work, but you could have been a plant. There is a lot we don't know about what's going on. We've told you about us, how about you fill us in on your story?"

Sora decided to give him a short version in the hope that she could change the subject. She could always elaborate later if necessary.

"Not much to tell. I was born in Seoul. My parents are both dead. Not too many friends. I've been doing some not great jobs while I work on my Tae Kwon-Do. Truthfully, this seems like the excitement I've been looking for."

RaeWon made his decision. "I'd like you to work with me. I can promise some excitement, some less exciting times, and training you won't get anywhere else. Yes?"

YeJin looked from RaeWon to Sora hopefully.

"Okay," said Sora, "when do we start?"

YeJin smiled and RaeWon said, "Right now." He turned to YeJin. "Let's get ready and call Ryu DaeHo to accept the work."

***

Ryu DaeHo sat at his desk, doing nothing. He was mentally

willing the phone to ring while simultaneously trying not to look concerned. He hadn't slept well last night and had finally got out of bed at 04:00 to go for a run. That hadn't seemed to help and neither did the numerous cups of coffee that followed. He knew that the encounter between his goons and Park YeJin could have gone better, but that was water under the bridge. *Move forward*, he told himself.

Would she call? Why hadn't she just accepted the proposal in the first place and saved everyone all this trouble? And why were they so insistent on using her. This in particular bothered him. He wasn't sure why he was so bothered, but something tugged at his mind and made him uncomfortable.

He picked up a piece of paper from the desk, made a ball out of it with his hands, and launched it at the waste bin. It went in, raising his spirits for a moment. Reality quickly returned and he wondered, not for the first time, why he had accepted his current assignment. Things had been so much easier just a few months ago.

The phone rang. He was startled and looked at it as though it had just bitten him. It rang three times, and then he answered it.

"Yes?" He cleared his throat.

"This is Park YeJin. I didn't appreciate the message last night, but I will accept the work. I'll need a standard requirements kit and materials. I'll do the work here at my studio."

All his self-doubt disappeared. Obviously he had made all the correct decisions so far and his bosses would be very happy with him. "Excellent, I'm glad you've came to our way of thinking. I'll courier the package over to you this afternoon. The original fee will be paid on completion and the deadline is four days."

"I thought you were doubling the fee?"

"That was before I had to go to the trouble of sending you the message last night. Four days."

He hung-up. After pausing for a minute to congratulate himself, he dialed his boss. "She has agreed."

There was a grunt in reply and his boss hung-up.

A huge weight had been lifted from his shoulders. He shrugged as though testing them and smiled to himself as a thought popped in his head. Time for an early lunch.

CHAPTER FIVE

The courier arrived with a box a few hours later. RaeWon and Sora stayed out of sight until YeJin was alone again. RaeWon handed a pair of thin latex gloves to YeJin and she pulled them on before placing the box on her desk. She sat and looked at it warily. It was a plain cardboard box, large enough to contain some file binders and the materials she would need. But what it contained triggered memories of a previous life. It seemed so long ago that she had left the NIS, or rather since they had left her. She wasn't traumatized by the end of her career and the embarrassment had faded over time; partly because she no longer saw any of her former colleagues and partly because she knew that she had not made an error in her work. The fact that RaeWon had stood by her had helped more than she could say.

Now that she thought about it, he was always there for her but never intruded. Her mind slipped away from the desk and she wondered if he was interested in her. Was she interested in him? It had been three years, wouldn't they have figured it out by now? She sat back and relaxed, ignoring the box.

RaeWon cleared his throat and said, "YeJin ... shall we open the box?"

She snapped back to reality and reaching for a camera on the desk, she handed it him. "Ready?" she asked.

He nodded and she faced the camera.

"My name is Park YeJin. Today is March 5 and it is just after 14:00. This is the box couriered over from Ryu DaeHo at the NIS. He said it would contain a requirements kit and materials for me to produce some international documents. I have no knowledge of the mission or the country where it will take place."

She slit the top open with a knife. Folding the top aside, she looked inside and saw the familiar tools of her former trade. One by one she removed them, laid them on the desk, and moved the box aside. She paused as she looked at the all too familiar items and the memories flooded back. Those had been good times, she thought. Her shoulders slumped imperceptibly as she recalled the last few days at the NIS, but she straightened and looked again at the items with a new focus. She continued her narration for the camera, indicating the items as she spoke.

"This binder will contain the project requirements and digital assets. These are the blanks for a British drivers license, credit cards, and a British passport. Unless there is something strange in the requirements, this seems to be a very small cover-job, probably for a quick entry-exit project."

YeJin opened the binder. Inside were the expected, and totally standard, NIS pages which specified the items to be prepared as well as the information about the recipient. One insert had pockets containing a USB drive, which she knew would contain any images needed.

Without looking up, she said, "RaeWon, this is a very small job." She read over the requirements. "One passport, one credit card, and one drivers license. Why didn't they do this in-house, it makes no sense."

Sora leaned forward. "What does this tell us?" she asked.

"Either this is an identity to supplement an existing one, or it is for someone being moved, or the agent will be undertaking a very short-term mission." He tapped YeJin on the shoulder. "Do we know this person?"

YeJin moved so he could see the page. "I don't think I have seen this one before. Perhaps it isn't an agent." She turned to look at RaeWon. "I'm just going to say this, because we've been thinking it but not saying it. This is an off-the-books operation and I'm a disposable player. Aren't I?"

Sora looked between the two of them with a puzzled look on her face and YeJin hoped she wasn't too scared.

RaeWon turned the camera off and nodded. "I think you're right about it being off-the-books. But there could be other reasons for not doing it themselves. There might be a leak in the operation and you were a safer option other than just shopping the job around town. It doesn't mean that you are disposable."

"Disposable?" asked Sora. "Like kitchen trash?"

RaeWon raised a hand. "Let's not panic. That is a very extreme possibility --"

"I'll remember that if it happens!" YeJin interrupted sarcastically.

"-- but it doesn't mean we won't plan accordingly," he continued, "so we need to find out everything we can about this mission."

YeJin smiled as Sora raised her hand to get RaeWon's attention.

"I know I'm new at this, but don't we become more dangerous to them when we know more?" she asked.

"Yes," he responded, "but only when they know that we know. If they think we don't know anything, then we become less dangerous."

"Unless knowing anything at all is dangerous," said YeJin.

"True," answered RaeWon, "but they only know about you and not us." He indicated himself and Sora.

"This gets better and better," muttered YeJin.

***

RaeWon and Sora left through the rear of the building, taking the USB memory with them.

"Where are we going?" asked Sora.

"To visit a friend and buy some gifts," RaeWon smiled. "Not too far away."

They walked across the alley and immediately entered another building, climbing the stairs to the top floor. RaeWon knocked on a door, stepped back, and waited. Sora looked up as RaeWon waved to the ceiling and saw a camera that she would not have seen on her own. The door opened slightly with a click as though someone had released it remotely. RaeWon pushed it open and she followed him inside to a space with a small table surrounded by four chairs and a window obscured by potted plants from floor to ceiling.

"In here, RaeWon," said a voice from another room.

The two of them followed the voice and found a man who Sora thought was nearer seventy than sixty. He was sitting at a workstation facing a bank of four computer monitors. Sora saw another monitor that displayed four camera views, including the alley they had just crossed and the doorway they had entered. RaeWon put a hand on the shoulder of the older man.

"How are you today, friend?" he asked.

"No complaints. Who is your friend?"

"This is Sora, my new partner. I'm taking her under my wing as a trainee."

The man stood and faced Sora, who bowed and extended a hand.

"Pleased to meet you," she said.

"RaeWon does not work with others easily, you must have impressed him." He turned to RaeWon and raised an eyebrow. "Did you have something for me?"

RaeWon produced the USB stick. "This is from the NIS. They are forcing YeJin to produce some documents for them. Obviously we are suspicious."

"Of course. I don't know why anyone would treat that nice lady in such a way, but I'm sure I won't like them if I meet them."

He took the memory and led them in to another room, full of computers. There was a red computer attached to a red keyboard, red mouse, and red monitor. His hands played over the keyboard and a program came to life on the screen. He looked carefully at the memory stick.

"Do you expect anything in particular?" he asked.

RaeWon shook his head. "No, we're just being careful."

"Very wise ..." He put the memory stick in to a port on the front of the computer and stood back. The screen displayed a string of characters. "Hmmm. This one is different from ones I've seen in the past."

"How?" asked RaeWon.

"Because of what is missing. I have never seen one that would allow the contents to be viewed on a computer outside of their control. This one is missing the files needed to prevent that." He clicked an icon and typed a command. "This device never had those files. If you were to ask my opinion I would say that this did not originate from the NIS."

RaeWon looked surprised.

"What does that mean?" asked Sora. "They knew that YeJin-shi would need the files, so isn't it natural?"

The man shook his head slowly. "In my experience, every device of this type that the NIS purchase has the files installed before it is allowed to be distributed for use."

"So whoever gave us this did not get it through regular channels," Sora suggested.

Both men were staring at the screen.

"Perhaps it was an oversight," said RaeWon.

"It is possible," said the man.

"But not likely?"

"No," the man agreed. "Highly unlikely."

He removed the device and handed it back to RaeWon. He smiled as he did so. "Please let me know when you have set a wedding date. I'm not getting any younger."

Sora noticed that RaeWon seemed a little flustered.

"You will be the first to know. And thanks for the information."

The man put a hand on RaeWon's arm. "Please...look after her. And Sora, too."

RaeWon nodded. "Let's go," he said to Sora. "We have one more stop to make."

***

RaeWon seemed lost in thought as Sora followed him out of the building, down the alley, and on to the main road to a bus stop. RaeWon looked around them as they waited for the bus but didn't say anything and Sora was content to wait in silence, too. A couple of minutes later the bus arrived, but instead of boarding, RaeWon stood aside to let everyone else pass him, then he walked away. Confused, Sora followed.

As they walked down the street, he turned to Sora.

"Lesson one. If someone had been following us, we would have seen them stop nearby, or wait with us. But if you do this, you are signaling that you know you might have a tail and also that you know enough to spot them. Better to not let people know you have any training whenever possible."

Sora nodded. Ten minutes later they entered a market and RaeWon made directly for an electronics shop.

"Wait across the street and do some window shopping, but keep an eye out so you can see when I leave. Then follow me and try not to let me know you're there," he told her and went inside.

Ten minutes later he had purchased three used cell-phones. The store employee put the phones in a plastic bag and handed it to RaeWon who paid with cash. RaeWon looked through the window to see if he could see Sora, but she was nowhere to in sight. He hadn't told her to hide, perhaps she was doing some shopping. Well, he would just leave her. This could be lesson two; pay attention.

He left the store and turned away from the direction from which they had arrived. He didn't look around but set off at a quick pace. A minute later he started to look for Sora, but she was still not in sight. He was a little disappointed that she had not followed his instructions, perhaps he had overestimated her. He exited the market and stood at a bus stop. Still no sign of Sora. He looked carefully in one direction, then turned to check the other direction. When he turned back, Sora was standing about ten meters away. She waved. He realized that she looked different, she had removed her jacket and was wearing a baseball cap with her hair in a ponytail.

RaeWon smiled and waved her over. Clearly he had not

underestimated her, but had overestimated himself. Lesson three was for him.

"I'm impressed," he told her, still smiling, "are you sure that you've never had any training?"

"I just did it," she said simply. "It was like an instinct."

RaeWon started to decide this was a rather arrogant answer, but the look on the her face told him she was being honest. "Good job," he said.

They left the bus stop and started to walk back to YeJin.

***

When they got back, YeJin was about to start work on the documents. All the blanks were arranged on her workspace and she was poring over the requirements to make sure all the details were clear to her. She was as methodical as she had always been, as if there had been no time away from this kind of work. The project seemed straight-forward and she felt as though she was ready.

She hardly looked up as RaeWon and Sora came in. RaeWon unpacked the cell phones and started to charge the batteries, while Sora found herself a bottle of water.

"How was the trip," asked YeJin, still not looking up.

"Good," said RaeWon. "I've got us some fresh phones and Sora showed me her talents at trailing a suspect."

"How was she?" YeJin was curious.

"Truthfully, a prodigy!" he looked over to Sora. He had accepted her story earlier, but she was too good not to have more to tell him. "You said it was instinct, but where do you think those skills came from?"

Sora thought for a moment before answering. The time she had spent with her uncle, doing the same things they had done today, was special and she didn't want to share it with anyone. Even people she was beginning to trust. She decided to open up just a little, especially as RaeWon seemed to suspect her claims of instinct.

"When I was a child, I would visit an uncle in Hong Kong and this was one of the games we would play."

RaeWon beckoned her over and signaled her to take a seat. This sounded a little strange to him. But he knew better than to push too hard for information. Although there weren't too many people that he knew who had been taught tradecraft at an early age. "Tell me your story," he said.

"Story ...?"

"Yes. I did a very cursory check on you, as you know, but the kind of skill you showed is hard to learn. Tell me about your family, and growing up."

"Well ... I was born in Seoul. My mother died during my birth and I was raised by my grandmother. I never knew my father, Grandmother would never talk about him. I don't think she knew him well. She and my mother had been estranged. I think I had a pretty normal childhood other than that ..."

"Except for Hong Kong," said RaeWon. "Tell me about that."

Sora wished now that she had not mentioned Hong Kong.

"I would go during the summer for a few weeks each year to stay with an uncle. I think I was five when I first went and the last time was when I was..." she furrowed her brow in thought, "... fourteen."

"Why did you stop?"

"My grandmother started to have poor health and I stayed to look after her. And I had friends in the neighborhood. I guess my priorities changed and I just stopped going."

YeJin had stopped what she was doing to listen to the story. "How is you grandmother?

Sora looked down. "She died when I was seventeen."

YeJin knew her face showed concern. "And you've been on your own since then?" she asked.

"I stayed with a friend's family for a couple of years and then moved out on my own. Practicing and studying TKD has taken a lot of my time."

RaeWon was satisfied for the moment. He looked at his watch. "I have to start a surveillance in a couple of hours, so I'll head over to my office to prepare. I'll see you two back here in the morning."

"Should I come with you?" asked Sora. "As your new employee."

"Not tonight. Get some rest and make sure YeJin doesn't go out to a club."

YeJin was startled. "What?"

They said their goodbyes and RaeWon left YeJin and Sora together. YeJin was thinking how well Sora had turned out considering her lack of a mother, having to care for a grandmother, and losing all her family at such a young age.

"I'm fine, don't worry," said Sora.

YeJin smiled and wondered if everyone could read her thoughts, "It seems so!"

CHAPTER SIX

March 07 | 10:00

Ryu DaeHo had given Park YeJin four days to complete the work. It took her two. When the job was done, RaeWon called a meeting of the three partners.

"So, YeJin, what do we know about the mission?" he asked.

YeJin had the documents arranged in front of her on the table in the kitchen and she looked them over to put her thoughts in order.

"The documents are for a woman. I don't recognize her. According to the package, she is 31 years old, her occupation is given as a teacher. I made a British drivers license and a credit card from a British bank."

"Did you make copies?" he asked.

"Yes."

Sora leaned over and touched the passport.

"That is a British passport issued to residents in Hong Kong before it reverted to the Chinese," said YeJin, pointing to the document. "The picture they supplied was created to look like an average passport photo, but this woman is not ordinary. I would guess that she is very good looking in person."

RaeWon picked up the passport, looked at the picture and

nodded in agreement. "Yes, they tried to hide that fact, but I think you're right. Very pretty."

YeJin took back the passport and placed it on the table. "I'll get you a copy of the photo if you're that interested," she said.

"Just professional curiosity," he protested.

Sora had got used to their bickering even in the short time she had known them and took it in stride.

"Anything else, YeJin?" asked RaeWon.

She shook her head. "No. Nothing left in there accidentally, no stamps requested from a recent trip. Assuming that the mission is in the UK, then she might be traveling from Hong Kong."

It was RaeWon's turn to shake his head. "Let's not assume anything, it could be anywhere in Europe. Did the NIS say how they wanted the documents sent to them?"

"I'm supposed to call when they are ready. Should I do that now?"

"No, we'll wait until nearer the deadline." RaeWon leaned back in his seat. "We need to decide what to do next."

"Next?" asked Sora. "Isn't it finished?"

"The best thing that can happen is that they pay YeJin and forget that she exists. But this operation seems as though it might be off-the-books, in which case the fewer people that know about it, the happier they will be."

"Is this where YeJin gets thrown out with the kitchen waste?" asked Sora.

"Well ... possibly," he said, looking at YeJin.

YeJin looked back and forth between the other two. "Let's make a plan that can't fail."

RaeWon smiled. "Naturally. But it will involve preparing to run. We should think about where we can go and what documents we'll need."

"We? Isn't it enough for just me to go?"

"It might," he replied teasingly, "but someone has to look after you!"

"Do you think they know we have kept in touch with each other?" she asked.

RaeWon shrugged. "I don't know, but I don't want to assume. We haven't broadcast that information, but if they ask around or check local cameras they might be able to put two and two together. And we have Sora to consider, too."

***

March 09 | 08:00

For the next two days, the three of them kept to their usual routine, as though nothing out of the ordinary had happened. YeJin worked on a couple of portrait assignments with Sora's help, and RaeWon was busy finishing a surveillance assignment for a client.

On the morning of the deadline, they were sitting around the table once again, ready to make and record what they hoped would be their final call to the NIS.

YeJin dialed the number and they listened to it ring four, five, six times. The call was answered by voice-mail and YeJin ended the call without leaving a message.

"Well, that was an anti-climax," she said. "I'm not sure what I was expecting, but that wasn't it. Maybe he hasn't had his coffee yet."

Before anyone could answer, the phone rang.

"Hello," said YeJin.

"*Is it ready?*" The voice was devoid of any emotion, as though the job was unimportant.

"Yes."

"*I will send a courier to pick it up. One hour.*"

The call ended.

YeJin broke the silence that followed. "That was more like what I was expecting."

"Is everything packed?" asked RaeWon, gesturing to the box that sat on the table.

"Just the finished items and the requirements package. I've kept the blank licenses and passport in case I ever need them. If he asks about them, I'll just say they were used for practice and have been destroyed."

"So, it's over?" asked Sora.

RaeWon shrugged. "I don't know. We'll stick to our plan, look out for each other, and see what happens. We'll be ready."

***

Later that same day the box containing YeJin's careful work was sitting in front of Ryu DaeHo. It had been opened and he looked down at the contents as he dialed his phone.

He lifted his head as the call was answered. "I have received the documents, sir."

"*Have them authenticated, quietly, through regular channels. Do not discuss them with anyone. No one is to know anything about this project. Is that clear?*"

He nodded. "Yes, I understand. Should I terminate the relationship?"

"*Not at this time. Our plans have changed somewhat. Pay her and let her know that there may be other work in the future. Include the bonus originally discussed.*"

"I will." He knew better than to argue, even though he had to fight to suppress his questions.

***

YeJin could not have been more surprised when the same courier who had picked-up the box that morning, appeared late in the afternoon with another box. This box was slightly smaller than the first and while she was afraid to open it, she did find the courage to shake it a little. Something moved inside but she had no clue what it could be. After staring at it for a while she carefully opened it, the whole time expecting it to explode. It didn't.

When she could eventually see inside, there was a letter and a block of something solid inside a white, plastic bag. YeJin opened the letter. It was short and had been printed from a computer. No signature.

"Thank you," she read, "we appreciate your work. Here is the money as discussed. There may be other small jobs in the future which we hope you will be interested in doing."

The letter, the fast payment, and the tone of the letter were completely unexpected. Not to mention that they were at complete odds with the NIS interaction so far. Her surprise increased when she counted the money. It included the higher amount which Ryu DaeHo had said would not be paid!

Perhaps she had misjudged them and the situation, she thought.

At that moment Sora walked in with a camera bag over one shoulder. She had shown interest during the portrait sessions and YeJin had encouraged her to take some walks and practice with the equipment. Sora saw the white plastic bag in front of YeJin.

"A gift?" she asked

In reply YeJin emptied the bag on to the table.

Sora looked at the money as it spilled out. "Do all your clients pay in cash?"

"No, but the NIS did."

CHAPTER SEVEN

March 16 | 19:45

Over the next week Sora started to develop a routine, spending some time with YeJin at the studio working with the cameras and lighting equipment, and switching with RaeWon as he introduced her to his work, another area that she was having fun with.

YeJin had insisted on sharing the NIS money equally between the three of them. Sora and RaeWon had protested that she had done the work, but YeJin pointed out that they had accepted the risk equally. Which was, as far as they knew, still ongoing. But nothing had happened and they all seemed to be feeling a little better about it each day. Secretly Sora wasn't convinced that the something they dreaded might be getting closer rather than farther away, but the other two seemed optimistic. And in Sora's opinion, they had far more experience than she did of these kind of things.

Seven days after their pay-day Sora was out with RaeWon while he worked a case. A medium-sized corporation had hired him to get some answers about an employee who they thought might be leaking information. RaeWon had been following the target for three days whenever he left his office. The target had done nothing unusual. Lunch with colleagues one day, a company dinner the next night. On the third night he had visited a shop and purchased lingerie.

RaeWon and Sora were looking at a map together when the man came out of the store, bags in-hand. RaeWon nodded to Sora and she started to follow him as he walked away. RaeWon followed Sora, carefully keeping a distance between them. A few minutes later the target had left the busy street and entered an alley. He entered a bar and Sora stopped at the door. RaeWon appeared a few moments later.

"He went inside. Are you going to go inside too?" she asked.

RaeWon nodded. "Wait out here, somewhere close. I'll call you if anything happens," he said, indicating the phone he had given her. He entered the bar and left Sora outside. She walked a short distance from the bar back toward the street and began her impression of a girl waiting for someone. With her phone plugged in to her ears she looked to everyone as though she were listening to music as she waited.

Inside the bar, RaeWon had mentally noted the time for his client report and looked around for the target. Occasionally glancing at his watch, he also looked like someone trying to find a friend. He located the target and sat at the bar where he could see both the target and the door with a minimum of head movement. The pretty girl behind the bar came over to him, dropping her towel on the counter on the way. She smiled genuinely at RaeWon and he leaned forward to order a drink. He looked around. The target was sitting alone at a table, bags on the floor, as a beer was placed in front of him. He picked it up and took a drink. There was only one drink so RaeWon didn't think he was going to meet anyone here. He seemed quite thirsty though as he finished the first beer and ordered another. Was he drinking for courage, RaeWon wondered.

The second beer was nursed longer than the first and twenty minutes later the target collected his belongings and left the bar without looking back. RaeWon had started to text Sora as soon as saw what was happening. She responded quickly.

Heading back to the road, she texted, *taking a taxi*.

By this time RaeWon was nearly at her location and could see her standing in a shadow. He saw the target get in to a taxi.

Sora had moved to the roadside and was stopping another taxi. As the first left, he hurried over and jumped in with her. He pushed some money at the driver.

"We'd like to follow our friend in that taxi," he said calmly, indicating the other car. "It's a game we play with each other."

The driver looked at the money, took it, and without saying a word started following in one fluid movement, as though everyone played this game. RaeWon and Sora sat in silence as the two cars threaded their way through the traffic. Their driver followed with ease and without making it obvious to the other car. RaeWon noticed that Sora was paying close attention to the technique and smiled to himself. He was impressed with his protégé.

It seemed that their journey was not going to be too long as they turned off the main road and followed the target up an alley and watched him disappear round a corner. As they rounded the corner they found the taxi stopped and the target getting out. Without being asked their driver managed to get past the other car and stopped around the next corner. They both quickly exited and without waiting, the taxi left. They made their way back toward the target and as they came into view, RaeWon took Sora's hand. He felt her stiffen in surprise and could sense that her whole body was reacting to the *skinship*.

"Sorry," he whispered, "just in case he sees us."

Sora nodded silently.

They needn't have worried as the target was oblivious to the world around him. They moved in to the shadows and stopped.

"Camera," whispered RaeWon.

Sora was already pulling the camera from her backpack. The combination of the Nikon D3 and 70-200 lens was not small, and in her small hands it looked even larger.

The target was standing in the street, straightening his tie while holding his bags. It looked very awkward. His body language gave the impression of a nervous man meeting a woman.

Sora had already selected a high ISO on the camera to allow for the darkness. He moved forward to a gate and opened it.

RaeWon made a note of the address. They heard the gate creak as it opened and Sora used the noise to cover the sound of the camera as she took some shots. At the door an outside light came on and he rang the bell. They saw him wave at the door camera. The door opened, light was added to the scene from inside and a woman appeared. Sora continued to take pictures. RaeWon thought that she seemed to be about ten years younger than the target.

The target lifted the bag as though offering it to the woman, who smiled and pulled him inside. The door closed.

RaeWon stiffened as he saw the glow from a cigarette further down the alley. He gently pulled Sora further back in to the shadow and hoped that they had been no glint on the camera lens from the light at the door. The exterior light went out automatically. The cigarette fell to the ground and RaeWon thought he heard the sound of a shoe rubbing the remains in to the concrete.

He leaned in to Sora and whispered, "We're not alone." He indicated the dark shape. Sora looked in that direction but couldn't see anything. Then she caught a slight movement. She nodded and slowly lifted the camera. A vehicle came down the alley and they pressed even closer to the building they were sheltered against. The headlights caught the shape by surprise, or he wasn't worried about it, and Sora was able to get a burst of shots. RaeWon motioned to put the camera away.

Putting the backpack over her shoulder they held hands again and walked away from the scene. As soon as they were out of sight, he let go of her hand.

"Good job," he said as they walked, "You're quite the natural at this sort of thing!"

Sora blushed a little at the praise. "Thanks."

Taking another route back to the road they caught another taxi back to RaeWon's office. Sora took the memory card out of the camera and loaded the images on to the computer, tagging them automatically as they were uploaded.

RaeWon was sitting at another computer writing down the details of the evening, ready for his report to the client. He opened another program and looked-up information on the house they had just been at. He printed the ownership information.

Having finished his work, he walked over to the small fridge and took out a bottle of water.

"Water?' he asked.

"Yes."

He took another bottle over to Sora as she finished the upload. He put it on the desk, next to her backpack. Something caught his eye on the pack and he turned it slightly to get a better view. Stitched on one of the pockets was a patch. He turned on a desk light and peered at the patch. He was surprised at himself that he hadn't noticed it before.

"Sora, this patch. How do you come to have it?"

Sora turned. "Oh, that? It brings me luck. I found it in my mothers belongings when I was young. There was a letter with it. Someone gave it to her for protection."

"Curious. Do you still have the letter?"

"Yes, do you want to see it? I can bring it tomorrow."

"I would be very interested. Look, it's getting late, I'll walk you back to the studio. Ready?"

She nodded, put the camera back in the backpack and was ready to go.

As they walked, she carefully asked, "Is it a coincidence that your office is so close to the studio?"

He was silent for a moment. "No, not really. I wanted to be able to keep an eye on YeJin."

"I understand," she said with an innocent look on her face.

"There is nothing to understand," he protested.

"I understand."

***

March 17

The next morning Sora was making breakfast when YeJin arrived.

"Breakfast?" she asked, pointing to the table. Before she got an answer RaeWon arrived.

"I have that letter," Sora told him.

"Letter?" asked YeJin. "Are you writing letters to each other now?"

"No," said RaeWon. "I'll tell you about it after I read it."

Sora fetched an envelope from her backpack and gave it to him. He sat at the table and took a sheet of paper out of the envelope. He read it for a couple of minutes then folded it and sat back.

"I don't believe it!" he said in disbelief. He looked at the two women. "This is unbelievable."

They were both curious, but knew better than to try and hurry an explanation from RaeWon. He saw the look on their faces.

"This letter was written to Sora's mother just before Sora was born." He lifted the backpack and showed YeJin the patch. "It came with that patch. Do you recognize it?"

YeJin looked at the patch, then at at Sora, and finally at RaeWon. "Yes. British SAS."

"Exactly. In 2007 I attended a lecture and demonstration by a former SAS soldier who was invited to speak. He was very impressive. We had some meals together and spent a couple of days visiting around Seoul. And he gave me one of these, too. Do you have a knife or scissors?"

YeJin produced a small knife and handed it to him. He took it and began to remove the patch from Sora's backpack. When he had removed it, he turned it over and found a number on the back.

"What is it?" asked Sora.

"This is the number that identifies that soldier to the British Army."

YeJin pointed at the patch. Do you think the same person gave one to her mother and one to you?"

"The name on the letter and the name of the man I met are the same, so I believe it was the same person."

Sora sat down. "Wow. How strange."

YeJin had taken the letter and read it. "How romantic! So he gave this to her so that she could get his help if she needed it."

She lowered the letter and looked at Sora carefully. "Is he your father?"

Sora shook her head and then stopped. "I don't think so, but I had never thought about it."

"What do you know about your father?" asked RaeWon.

Sora stood and walked to the sink They were heading in to an area she didn't want to discuss. "Almost nothing. Grandmother wouldn't speak about him. I think she knew about him but didn't want me to know. The only thing she said was that he was a bad man."

"Not how I would describe this man," said RaeWon. "Did she ever mention a man that helped your mother just before your birth?"

Sora shook her head. "She almost never talked about my mother or my birth."

A silence fell on the group as they were lost in their own thoughts.

"Ah," said RaeWon. "There is one thing I remember about him. He had a Korean wife, someone he met about the time that he knew your mother."

Another, more awkward silence engulfed them.

RaeWon spoke again. "I have an idea. Our next training project will be to find him. What do you think?" He looked expectantly at Sora.

Sora wasn't sure about this. "To contact him?"

"Perhaps. I wouldn't mind being in touch with him again and we could ask about the story behind the letter." RaeWon became thoughtful as he remembered back to his days with the NIS. "I started to get involved with international operations after we met so a lot of the time I wasn't even being myself. It was hard to keep in touch with people."

YeJin motioned to RaeWon with her eyes that they should talk. "I want your advice on something. Sora, we'll be back in a minute or two."

YeJin and RaeWon left the studio and he followed her across the alley to a mart. She looked over some drinks for a moment, then turned to him.

"Have you considered what will happen if this man is her father? Do you know if she even wants to meet him if that is the case?"

RaeWon looked a little downcast. "No, I hadn't thought about that ..."

"Exactly. You see a puzzle and want to solve it. Don't forget that she is still young. She may seem strong, but she is still young. Slow down a little. Okay?"

He nodded. "You're right."

***

Most people who knew RaeWon considered that one of his best attributes was the ability to follow a puzzle to the very end. And the connection between Sora and this man from his past would not leave his mind, despite YeJin's warning. The more he thought about the puzzle, the less he remembered her words.

Later that same day Sora was with him at his office looking at the pictures from the surveillance.

"Is this a girlfriend?" she asked.

RaeWon looked up from his computer. "Possibly. Probably. Let me show you how we research this."

Sora dragged her chair over and sat next to him.

"This is the ownership information on the house where he met the woman," he pointed at two sheets of paper, "and this is a list of companies that our client suspects of receiving information. The house is owned by this person," he indicated a name, "so see if you can find that name associated with any of these companies." He handed the lists to Sora and she returned to her own computer.

RaeWon started to rummage around on his desk, lifting papers to see what lay underneath and generally moving everything around. He checked a drawer and pulled out a large stack of business cards which he had collected over the years. The cards were held together by a rubber band, which broke as soon as he tried to remove it, letting the cards fall to the desk.

Sora looked over at the sudden flurry of noises. "Do you want me to tidy the desk for you?" she asked.

"No, no. Have you found anything yet?"

She shook her head and went back to her work.

RaeWon collected the cards and started going through them. He knew that he had collected a business card from the man in Sora's letter, but he couldn't remember where he had put it. Although an excellent field agent, the transition to entrepreneur had not been easy. Being your own boss sounded so good, but for RaeWon the reality of finding clients, invoicing them, and writing reports, had taken the shine off self-employment. His filing system wasn't everything that it should be, which Sora had quickly noticed. Despite her offering to help on several occasions he had never accepted.

He worked his way through all the cards with no success. He put a new band around them and consigned them back to the drawer. He opened another drawer and there was the sound of something metallic as it moved. He reached in and brought out a small metal box. He laid it on his desk and took removed lid, revealing some mementos from his NIS days. Two passports lay on top, ones he had never returned and which were probably long-since canceled by his former employer. A few notes of foreign currency lay underneath. At the bottom was a patch. The patch.

"Sora, do you have the patch with you?"

She dug in her backpack and handed it to him. He turned it over in his hands and noted the number, comparing it to the one that lay in the box.

"Did you find your patch?" asked Sora. She got up and walked over, looking over his shoulder. Without saying anything, he showed her the two numbers, which were the same.

"Are you going to look for him?" she asked.

"YeJin said I should be careful," he answered.

"She has sense. But I don't think he is my father, if that is her concern. The letters seem to say that they had just met, but my mother was already about to give birth. And I'm curious about the story too."

RaeWon reached under the patch and pulled out a business

card. "This is his card. Let's see if the company still exists." He pulled the keyboard and mouse toward him and entered the web address from the card. The company website appeared on the screen. It was in English, of course, but RaeWon remembered enough to click on 'About Us', and then 'Our People'. Sora had matched the name on the card with the name on the screen next to the first photograph. She pointed to it.

"Is this him?"

RaeWon sat back. "Yes, almost exactly as I remember."

"How should we contact him?"

"How is your English?" RaeWon asked. "Mine is not as good as it used to be."

"I've never tried it with a person outside of school. How did you communicate before? You said he has a Korean wife, doesn't that mean he speaks Korean?"

"He spoke some Korean. My English was better then. We managed." He thought about it for a moment "We could email him. What do you think?"

"That should work and be a lot less awkward than us trying to communicate with people before we get through to him."

They navigated their way to a 'Contact Us' page and RaeWon started a message:

Clive, this is Jung RaeWon who you met when you visited the NIS to lecture some years ago. I would like to speak with you again on a personal matter. Please contact me.

He added his phone number to the end and sent the message.

"What time is it there?" asked Sora.

"About eight hours behind us. But I wouldn't expect a fast reply. He is probably busy or traveling."

Sora went back to matching the name of the homeowner against employees of the companies on the list.

***

The phone rang. RaeWon idly reached out and answered it

without looking at it.

"Hello - - Yes, how can I help you? - - Yes, of course." He reached for a desk diary. He hadn't written much in it so he looked at the ceiling to help him guess when he was available. "Wednesday, 14:00? - - I look forward to it. Thank you."

He replaced the phone.

Sora didn't look up from her work. "Write it down."

RaeWon opened his mouth to say something to his junior, but realized that she was right and thought better of it. He made a note of the appointment in the diary.

The phone rang again. RaeWon answered it again.

"Hello - - Yes, yes!" RaeWon stood and bowed. Sora couldn't fail to sense his excitement. "Yes, I met your husband in 2007 here in Seoul. We ate together several times when he was here and he mentioned you frequently - - I understand. It was kind of you to call and let me know - - The reason I called? ... yes ..."

RaeWon suddenly realized that YeJin might had been right to ask him to slow down. How could he tactfully raise the subject of another woman with this man's wife? He didn't have enough information to make his way through this minefield.

"I came across the gift that he left me, a badge cap from his military unit - - Yes, an SAS cap badge - - To special people only? I'm honored." He decided to continue carefully with his story. "I also met a person who received one from him during a previous visit to Korea. There is a letter with it and I was hoping to ask him about the story behind it - - The letter? Well, it was to a lady - - Yoo Eun-Hee? Yes! How did you know? - - Really? - - How did I meet her if she is dead? Well..."

He started to be unsure of himself again, but decided to forge ahead.

"I have met her daughter ..." He held the phone away from his head as an astonished scream came out of it. Sora, too, looked astonished, with so many questions that she wanted to ask. "Are you all right? - - I know it must be a shock. Truthfully, I only expected your husband to call. Hello? Hello?"

He looked at Sora. "The line is dead."

"What happened?" asked Sora.

Without answering, he called YeJin. "YeJin! Can you come over to my office? - - Yes, now." He hung up. "Let's wait until YeJin gets here, okay?"

Sora could barely contain her curiosity. She had never seen RaeWon this agitated. And why call YeJin over with no notice?

RaeWon paced the floor for ten minutes until YeJin's head appeared in the doorway. He silently waved her in and directed her to a chair while he remained standing.

"What have you done?" asked YeJin gently.

Sora took her usual position when the three of them were together, of looking between the other two. Their sibling-like interaction was usually entertaining, but this time her curiosity was ready to burst out.

"Do you remember your last words when you suggested I slow down about the letter?"

"Yes," YeJin said slowly.

"Well, I ... I mean *we* ...", he corrected quickly, pointing to Sora.

"Don't blame Sora. What have you done?"

"I'm trying to tell you. I ... *we* ... sent a message to his company asking him to get in touch --"

"And ...?"

"And his wife called." RaeWon waited for YeJin to explode.

Sora wondered why someone she had heard was so good in the field as an agent could turn in to this person in front of YeJin.

YeJin merely closed her eyes. "How did it go?"

"Considering I told her that I had met someone she thought died twenty years ago, I think it went pretty well. Until the line went dead."

"Tell us everything," demanded YeJin, who was getting curious too.

"When our message arrived they asked her to translate it. She said that her husband is on a trip at the moment and will return tomorrow." RaeWon gave YeJin a meaningful look and turned to Sora. "His wife knew your mother, in fact they were best friends. She seemed very shocked ..."

Sora put her hand to her mouth as she gasped. YeJin saw tears start to form in her eyes and realized why RaeWon had called her over. She went over and put an arm around Sora, who was clearly shocked at the memory of a mother she had never known coming to sudden life. A time of her life which had always been grey in her mind, now taking on color.

RaeWon, used to working alone and out of his depth in this kind of situation, maintained his distance.

The phone rang.

Everyone looked at it.

RaeWon answered the call.

"Hello - - Yes, I understand. I'm sorry to give you the news in this way - - No, no, I was wrong - - She is safe. We're working together and she is staying with a lady friend of mine - - You are kind. Don't worry, we feel the same way - - Yes, I look forward to greeting him again - - Goodbye."

He turned back to the room to find the girls staring at him. They didn't have to ask.

"She was shocked and dropped the phone, which cut the call. She has spoken with her husband and they both want to make sure Sora is safe. They said they feel like they have rediscovered a lost daughter. Anything Sora needs, they will take care of it."

Sora thought about this for a moment and was overcome by the fact that people she had never met instantly considered her family. It was happening so quickly. Meeting YeJin and RaeWon, who had taken her in. And now these people overseas. She had suddenly gone from someone with no family or friends, to having people who had never met her but cared so much. Her life seemed to be changing and she was not in control. It was overwhelming. She put her head down and started to cry quietly. YeJin wrapped her arms around her again.

RaeWon was still curious about the rest of the story.

Chapter Eight

June 03 | 07:00

Two months had passed in a blur for Sora. Her time was now spent primarily with Jung RaeWon as he continued and intensified her training. She enjoyed the work and the puzzles almost as much as he did, and he seemed happy with her progress.

As she sat at the table, the plate of peeled fruit growing slowly in front of her, she decided that her life had taken a turn for the better and she was happy with the path she seemed to be on. RaeWon and Park YeJin both looked after her well and soon she would be on a flight to England to meet Clive and his wife, Song EunJae. Song EunJae, who had been her mother's best friend, had been overjoyed at the prospect of being reunited with Sora who she had not seen since Sora's birth. They had spoken on the phone half a dozen times since discovering each other. The calls were awkward as Sora did not really understand why these people considered her like family. This lack of comprehension was mainly because she had not had any close friends in her life and everyone that had been close had left her. At school there were people who tolerated her, but no one really close. Her first, and only, boyfriend turned out to be not such a nice person. That was six months ago now, but she still shuddered inside at the memory. Sora did not think she had felt alone growing up, but now that there were so many people around her, she realized that she had actually been very lonely. She smiled as she selected a piece of pear and ate it. Life felt good now.

RaeWon appeared in the doorway.

"You seem happy," he said.

"I am," she nodded. "Today is my first solo surveillance, right? Any changes to the plan?"

"No, everything is the same. Let's go over it one last time."

Sora fetched the mission file from her room and they sat at the table. RaeWon opened the file. He indicated the photograph clipped to a sheet of paper.

"This is our target. He is meeting one or more people who are interested in buying information from him."

"Who arranged the meeting?"

"He did, which is how we know where it is taking place. My contact at the hotel is going to make sure that a specific room is used so that you can monitor the meeting."

"From another building."

"Yes. You will be on the roof of a building to the South of our target, at a distance of less than forty meters. I need you to take photographs and video. Which camera are you taking?"

"The D3 with the 200-400 F4 lens. No audio?"

"No, no audio. Our client is content just to see the people involved at the meeting." RaeWon was always very serious when briefing. "We've visited the building and you know where you are going. The guard will let you on to the roof after you meet him at the rear entrance that we looked at."

Sora nodded.

"Double, triple check your equipment before you leave. Allow time to get there early. The meeting is at 20:00. I know this isn't international espionage, but remember rule number one. The people you can see are not always the only ones in the game. And please don't fall off the roof."

Sora smiled to reassure him.

"I'll be available by phone all day. Any questions or concerns, call me," he concluded.

"So this is what having a mother sounds like?" she asked.

"Would you rather hear YeJin's lecture on safety?"

Sora raised her hands in mock horror. "No, no, no. I've listened well."

"Did I hear my name?" YeJin walked through the door and put her bag on the table.

"He won't stop talking about you," teased Sora.

"When did I do that?" RaeWon protested.

"All he does is talk." YeJin took a piece of fruit. "Are you ready for today?" YeJin took a bite and waived the fruit at Sora. "I'm sure you are. Just don't fall off the roof."

***

17:00

Sora looked out of the window of the taxi as it made its way quickly north toward Seoul Plaza. The mist from the morning had been replaced with a haze which had lost out to a partly cloudy sky. The people outside the window were on their way home, or to office dinners, or another meeting. Wherever they were heading she doubted that many of them were on their way to sit on a rooftop with a camera. Looking again at the sky, rain did not seem to be on the menu. This was good news.

The taxi moved out of the traffic and slid to a stop against the wide concrete walkway bordering the large egg-shaped area of grass that is Seoul Plaza. Immediately a small group formed to see who could be the next customer for the taxi. Sora paid with her transport card, thanked the driver, and left the vehicle. Backpack over one shoulder, she paused for a minute to take in the hustle and bustle around her. She felt like she was in a large video game, the only one really alive, everyone else extras in her movie.

She took out her phone and sent a text message. A moment later a reply came. After reading the message she turned the sound off on the phone. As she did so, she wondered if she were really alone on the mission, or if RaeWon was nearby watching her. She glanced around but didn't see him. She turned and started walking to the south end of the Plaza, becoming part of the background to everyone else's movie.

The crowd crossed the road and when they reached the subway entrance on the other side, Sora broke free and turned left between two tall buildings. The narrow street was lined with black limousines. She rounded the building to her right and waited at a delivery entrance. Almost immediately the door opened from inside and a man appeared. RaeWon had introduced them a few days ago when he showed her the building. Sora wordlessly handed him an envelope and produced a stuffed bear from her backpack.

"For JiHyun."

She handed the bear to the man who bowed and took it.

"Thank you, she will love it!"

His previous icy demeanor gone, they entered the building and he led her to a freight elevator, which they boarded. The elevator took them to as close to the top of the building as it would go and they got out, using stairs for the remaining two flights to reach a locked door. The guard had a bunch of keys hanging from his belt and one opened the door.

Sora stepped through and looked around. The roof was covered with pipes and box-like obstructions. Around the edge ran a track for the window-washing equipment. She looked back and saw the helicopter landing pad. The guard waved the bear to say goodbye and disappeared. Sora took some tape from the backpack and using a thin piece of metal plate, she made sure that the door latch would not lock and leave her stranded on the roof. That done, she closed the door so that the alarm indicator in the guard-room would go out.

She stood for a moment and looked around, trying to mentally blend with her surroundings. Moving to the north-east corner of the building she put down her backpack and brought out the camera and lens. A memory card went in to the camera and she mounted the lens on the body. At the edge, really just a meter-high barrier to help hide the ugliness of the roof from below, a look toward the building to the north confirmed that the room was visible. A discrete 'X' had been marked in the corner of the window to help her locate it. Small enough for her to see with the telephoto lens, but not large enough to draw attention from within the room.

Sora looked at her watch: 17:30. Two and half hours until the meeting. She wouldn't normally have worn a watch, but RaeWon said a phone would put out too much light for a night surveillance. She selected a place to sit and pulled a bar of chocolate from her backpack. Breaking off a piece she savored the taste as she sat back to wait.

***

18:30

An hour later, a text message arrived. Sora felt the phone vibrate in her pocket. Bringing it out, the message was from RaeWon.

In position? All OK?

Yes, she answered.

The phone went back in her pocket. Looking at the sky, Sora saw an aircraft climbing higher in to the sky on its way to ... somewhere. She thought about her trip to England. Another two days and she would be on her way. She had often dreamed of traveling the world to exotic places. Perhaps one day when she met a special person, they could go together. She scowled in the evening light. What was she thinking? Hadn't she learned anything from life so far? Those special people were for dramas and other people.

Time to take another look around.

She crawled over to the camera and practiced taking some shots of the room and then started to look around at the surrounding buildings. There was a building to the east, the same distance from the target building, but about three times as far from her location. She panned around the roof. As she moved the camera, a movement caught her eye. She panned back but didn't see anything now. Must be a building guard on his rounds. As long as he didn't see her, that would be no problem.

Curiosity kept her looking. Making sure she was not silhouetted against the sky, she continued panning. There it was, another movement. Instinctively she took a photo. The camera sounded loud and she wondered if it could be heard a hundred meters away. The person on the other roof was climbing to the top of one of the structures on the roof. Obviously to get a better view, thought Sora, but of what? She kept taking photos. She saw a backpack on the climber's back. When the person reached their destination, they stopped and took off the backpack, then took some items from the pack and put them on the roof. A sudden gust of wind, seemingly from nowhere, blew the cap off the climber's head. As he reached up to try and catch it, this silhouetted him against the sky and Sora was able to take a photo with the climber looking almost directly toward her.

She lowered the camera and looked at the image on the back, zooming-in. It was a woman, and definitely not a security guard. Why would anyone be on the roof? Then it occurred to her that *she* was on a roof, so perhaps the other woman was there for a similar reason.

Check the time: 18:45.

Check the target room: no activity.

Sora trained the camera back on the other roof. The woman seemed to be putting something together and was apparently unaware of her presence. Sora watched her finish assembling the object and the hairs on the back of her neck began to stand up.

It was a gun.

The woman lay on the roof, the gun barrel supported by two legs. Sora suddenly realized, with some concern, that the gun was pointing at her roof. Not directly at her location, but obviously at her roof.

A buzzing sound began to get louder and it became more of a chopping or slapping sound. Behind her, the lights around the heli-pad came alive. From the north, the sound was getting louder. She searched the sky for the source and saw it as a bright light on the nose of the helicopter was suddenly turned on. Sora felt very exposed by the lights behind her, the light flying toward her, and the noise. She took some photos of the helicopter and turned back to the other roof.

She felt certain that all this light would give her away, but the woman was following the helicopter with her gun. Sora set the camera to record some video.

The noise completely enveloped her as the helicopter passed slowly overhead and transitioned to a hover about a meter above the landing zone. She shot some video of the helicopter as it came in to land.

It sat for a moment above the center of the heli-pad and then gently settled on to the pad. As soon as it touched down, a door opened on each side and three men jumped out. Three, fit men. Still shooting video, Sora saw the three look around for a moment and then signal to someone in the helicopter.

A fourth man slowly appeared, and joined them on the roof.

Sora didn't hear a shot, but saw the fourth man stop suddenly, stagger back a step as another bullet went though his neck, and then collapse backwards. The others gathered around him, but too late to protect him.

Turning back to the woman with the gun, Sora continued to video the scene as she saw a flash from the gun each time the next three shots were fired. Something must have reflected on her camera lens, she wasn't sure what happened, but the shooter turned the gun in her direction and snapped off another shot. It missed Sora, but hit the rail slightly in front and to one side of her. Bits of wood and metal flew up and were caught on the video.

This jerked Sora back to reality.

She had to get out of there.

She crawled to her backpack. Removing the lens from the camera she put them both in the pack. She looked around for anything she might have forgotten. Nothing lying around.

To leave meant that she would have to move toward the helicopter. If those men saw her, there was gong to a whole lot of trouble. Keeping low, she headed for the doorway back to the real world, the one where people were going about their lives as if nothing had happened two hundred feet above their heads.

Ten feet to go and one of the men saw her. Raising his gun he fired two quick shots in her direction. They missed. She kept moving, more quickly now, as the other men turned to find her.

Three more shots landed close by, but nothing hit her. She reached the door, pulled it open, ripped the tape and metal plate off the lock, and slammed it behind her. Without pausing she headed for the elevator. Was that too obvious? She pressed the button for the basement, and jumped out as the doors closed.

Her instinct was to hide until everything was over and then sneak out of the building. But she knew that the police would probably be all over the building very soon. She had to get out now.

She remembered YeJin's and RaeWon's warning about not falling off the roof and she almost laughed. That was the least of her problems.

CHAPTER NINE

June 03 | 18:30

The woman was in a hurry and she wasn't a person who liked to be in a hurry. She had a strong conviction that this was when people started making mistakes, and mistakes killed people. Of course, killing people was her job, but she much preferred to be the one doing the killing over being caught out of position or inadequately briefed.

The job she was on her way to perform had been a last minute change to her careful plans. The target was arriving at a different location and at a different time. If she didn't need to finish this job so much, she would have put a bullet though the client's head and gone home. The NIS dragging her out of recent retirement had been bad enough, but the manner in which they had done it was what had made her so bitter toward them.

But this had to be done.

Which is why she found herself climbing to the roof of a building in downtown Seoul.

A few minutes later she was on the roof. Taking a moment to get her bearings, she chose a vantage point on top of a structure. The structures around it, although not much higher, would give her some concealment from surrounding buildings. Looking over to the building to the west, she could see the heli-pad. She started climbing and was quickly at the top. Shrugging off her backpack, she brought out the pieces of her rifle. She glanced at her watch. Not much time left.

A gust of wind blew her cap off. She stretched to reach out for it, but missed. Her hair fell down around her face. She put it in a ponytail as fast as she could and lay down on her stomach. Extending the bi-pod at the end of the barrel, she sighted on the heli-pad. An excellent view.

She heard the helicopter approach, saw the landing lights flicker on at the heli-pad, and watched the aircraft descend gently to a landing. The men dropped out of the doors and she waited for her target.

There he was. She checked the settings on the scope, made an adjustment, and aimed. She squeezed the trigger and he staggered. Another shot and he was down. Three more shots kept everyone around the helicopter busy and guaranteed that any medical attention would be a little longer in being called. Every second helped.

A flash caught her eye. There it was again, slightly to the right. She turned the scope toward the flash and caught a slight movement, but it wasn't easy to make out any detail. Then she could see a head poking out above a low wall. What had caused the flash? Then she saw the camera lens. This was her worst nightmare. Witnesses were always a problem, but witnesses with cameras were a big problem. You never knew if they were taking still photos or video, not that either was good news. Coupled with not knowing if they were transmitting live back to another location and things were going from bad to worse. She cursed the contract she was on and the people she was working for.

Had she been set up? Was that why the plan had allegedly changed, so that she wouldn't have enough time to spot a set up?

Focus! Fix the problem and clean up the loose ends later.

She fired one shot, slightly low in the hope that the wall was not solid. She saw the impact and some debris rose in to the air. She cursed the whole situation again and began to take the gun apart, putting the pieces in to the backpack. She quickly checked for the ejected casings, collected what she found and started to leave. She had to find that photographer before the police arrived and the whole block became a danger zone. Quickly, quickly!

This had to be a set up. She had almost no time to get ready for the mission and now no time to grab the photographer.

She heard gun shots from the other roof. She jumped down from the structure. Reaching in the backpack she brought out a scope. On the other roof she could see the men. They were not looking in her direction, but seemed to be firing at a target on the same roof. They must have seen the photographer, she thought. Perhaps they would do her job for her. No, even if they got the photographer, they would still have the camera. Again, she cursed her employer and promised herself that their next conversation would be very interesting and on her terms.

The next step was obvious: get the photographer, or at least get enough information to allow him to be found later. She left the roof and started down the stairs. At the exit she raised her hood to cover her head and pushed the door open. The evening street sounds were momentarily distracting and she forced herself to concentrate on her surroundings, all the time moving away from the building. Standing with her back to the adjacent building gave a good view of the back of the building the photographer was on. She gambled that she had beaten him to the street and decided to wait until it looked like the police were arriving. This was a risk she had to take. Reputation is everything. No one hires an assassin who's photo has been on the front page of a newspaper. If the pictures were for blackmail by her employer, that was bad enough. Her personal business standards did not permit such activity and the penalty was final. Very final.

Why else would a photographer be on the roof, at exactly the right time and right place to interfere. She felt her anger rising and forced herself to be calm. This whole project was messing with her head.

Calm, be calm.

Chapter Ten

June 03 | 18:55

Sora made her way as quickly and as silently as possible down the stairs. She tightened the straps on the backpack as she went. YeJin would want the camera back, certainly, but would it be better to hide it somewhere and take only the memory card with her? Still descending the stairs she thought carrying five kilograms less would not be a bad thing, especially if she had to fight. Or run. She stopped and digging in her pack she removed the memory card. Where to put it? She settled for a pocket in her jeans. Content with her choice, she continued the descent. The sixteen floors seemed endless and what waited at the bottom was uncertain. The shooter had clearly seen her, but would she try to leave the area too, or would she try and find Sora?

Sora decided that if she had seen the camera, she would almost certainly try to intercept her. She would work on that assumption. If she was carrying the rifle, that would slow her a little, right? Perhaps, but no one was shooting at the assassin. She quickened her descent. Should she exit the way she had come in to the building? No, that was closer to the shooter. No point in making it easier for her. She remembered that there was a subway entrance outside the west entrance of the building. If she could get from the building to the subway without being seen, she might have a better chance. But wouldn't the shooter think the same way? She forced herself to stop second-guessing every decision. Sometimes, she thought, you just have to do something, right or wrong. At the third floor she left the stairs and worked her way to find a stairwell on the southwest corner of the building.

This building was starting to feel like a prison. She realized that she was in danger of panicking. But as soon as she acknowledged that, the feeling slowly started to subside.

She found the next stairway easily and didn't bump in to any cleaning staff or guards on the way. The ground floor and main entrance was in front of her a minute later.

Pausing to collect herself before rushing out, she leaned against the wall and brought out her phone. She badly wanted to contact RaeWon, but decided her time would be better spent leaving the area. The phone went back in her pocket. She thought that RaeWon would be handling this much more coolly than she was, but then he had done this kind of thing many times before. The whole situation made her think back to Hong Kong and the games she had played with her uncle. The memory gave her strength, but she still felt like she was taking a national exam without enough preparation. But there's a first time for everything, so she took a deep breath to focus herself. Of course, if you failed this test there was no re-take. Sora put a headset in her ears as if she were listening to music.

Composed and with a plan in mind, she stepped out of cover and walked confidently toward the entrance, the street visible beyond. She could see her target, the subway sign outside. Trying to look as though she had every right to be in the lobby at this time, she stole a look outside for the shooter or anyone who looked like they might do her harm. All clear. The people streaming past the exit were in groups and she timed her exit to coincide with one of them for cover. She pushed the door open without breaking her stride. Walking, walking, looking, walking, looking. Four meters to go. Three. Two. At the edge of her vision, a figure to her right at the corner of the building, near the other subway entrance. Backpack, pony-tail, and dressed in black, as was Sora. She seemed to be watching, trying to cover two directions at the same time.

Avoid her eyes she told herself, avoid her eyes. She tried to look away but couldn't. One meter to go. The shooter looked over and their eyes met. Shit! Sora's heart missed a beat, maybe two, but she kept moving. When she reached the subway entrance she went down three steps, and crouched down. She knew she had been spotted and that these stairs were met at the bottom by stairs from where the shooter was standing. It was time to gamble. As she crouched, Sora counted to three as slowly as she could, then ran back up the steps and walked quickly away from the subway exit, putting a group of people between them. A hundred meters ahead there was a road intersection. She continued south without looking back.

The gamble was that the shooter had entered the subway and was looking for her underground. And if she didn't descend to the train level, that she would at least be on the other side of the busy street. Sora decided she needed to head east to put a little more distance between them, then find somewhere to hide and call Jung RaeWon.

She was now a few blocks south of the building and a parking garage appeared on her left. She pushed through the low bushes and over the barrier. Once inside she hid in a spot where she could see if she was being followed. She dialed RaeWon.

***

Jung RaeWon was just finishing his meal when the phone vibrated. He glanced at the screen.

"It's Sora," he said to himself. "Hello, how - - Are you sure? - - Okay, Okay. Slowly, slowly."

"Yes, keep all the equipment with you. Have you taken the card out of the camera? - - Good - - You should keep moving, but is your location safe for a short time? - - Do you remember how to transmit a picture? Good. Send the best full-face photo you have to YeJin - - Now listen, be very, very careful. People who go around doing this kind of thing are professionals and you are now on their radar as a problem. Remember, just because you've seen one person, doesn't mean that there are aren't others as well. Send the picture. Stay hidden. Bye."

He ended the call, noted the time, and dialed YeJin.

"It's me - - Sora is in trouble - - No, she's not hurt yet, but only because of luck - - Listen - - She not only witnessed an assassination, but she is right in the middle of it. And she has video of it. She was fired at by both sides, but wasn't hit. She left the building, but needs to get further away before the police start closing streets. The good news is that they will take a while. She's in cover, but we absolutely can not assume that she is clear of a tail. She's good, but this is real life, not a game. When you get a photo from her, see if you can identify the shooter and call me - - Yes, I'm on my way to help her - - Call me when you've seen the picture."

RaeWon took some money to the counter and then hurried outside, heading for his office which was nearby.

Climbing the stairs to his office, a call arrived from YeJin. She was frantic.

"- - Calm down - - YeJin, take a breath. What is the matter? Did you get the photo? - - It's who? - - The woman in the documents!" RaeWon cursed. "Sorry, sorry. Are you sure? - - Okay, I understand. Let me think for a minute. Look, I'm just at my office now. I'll call you in two minutes, I've got to think about this."

He hung up on YeJin and opened the door to his office. Moving to a corner, he picked out his emergency bag which contained useful items for when you were having trouble in the field. He double checked the contents to make sure everything was there. It was. He turned to his safe and opened it. From inside he took out a 9mm pistol and three extra magazines. These items went in to the bag. Back at the safe, he removed his passport and two bundles of currency.

He wasn't sure exactly what he was planning for, but he had a very bad feeling about it. Was it a coincidence that the same person YeJin had been coerced in to producing documents for was the same woman that had just killed someone in front of Sora?

He dialed YeJin.

"I want you to do something for me. Make travel arrangements for the three of us. - - International. Sora to Hong Kong and book you and I to Australia and Japan - - As soon as possible, but it doesn't matter, we're not going to use them. If the NIS are involved then I want to keep them guessing about our intentions - - Use the card I gave you - - Then I want you to get your passport and any cash you have, we will have to hide out for a short while until we figure this out. And get the same for Sora. - - When you have finished, meet me at Gate Eight at Namdaemun market - - Yes, west side next to the police station. I'll have Sora meet us there, too..." He paused and there was silence over the line. "YeJin, you may not have much time. Do this quickly and get out of there."

Looking around, he didn't see anything else he wanted to take, so he closed the safe, locked the office door and went downstairs to find a taxi.

Why couldn't she have just fallen off the roof, he wondered, there would be a much better chance of survival.

Chapter Eleven

June 03 | 19:00

Kim JiMin was conflicted.

Not about whether shooting the man on the roof was right or wrong, she had no particular feelings one way or the other about that. Business is business. She accepted that taking a life was generally considered wrong by people, but also knew that you shouldn't judge a contract unless you have all the information. And sometimes no one has all the information.

No, her conflict was about the situation she found herself in. Was it caused by fate, her employer, or someone else? And exactly what was her situation? Not knowing was a cause of concern for someone used to planning the smallest detail. This was an entirely new and unsettling feeling.

She had seen the photographer exit the building and enter the subway. It had been impossible to tell if she was hunting a male or female, not that it made much difference in the end, but the quarry was now in her grasp. And she knew it was a woman. She quickly moved to intercept her at the bottom of the stairs. When that didn't work, she crossed under the street toward the entrance to the trains, trying to find her quarry in the crowd. Still no sign of her, so she went back up to street level. This photographer seemed to have some skills. Of course, it might be the luck of an amateur, but as a professional she knew never to underestimate an opponent.

At street level, now on the opposite side of the street, she ran south to the intersection. Once there she scanned the other side of the road. As luck would have it, she thought that she had her in sight again. Feeling inside her jacket for the pistol in the shoulder holster, she felt ready for action. She crossed the street continuing south, wanting to get ahead of her prey. As the light changed and the thick traffic stopped, the photographer was moving again.

Two blocks later she watched as the photographer disappeared in to a parking garage. Would she stop and hide? Or make her way through the garage to another street?

What should she do? It was so uncomfortable not to know what was happening. Think, she thought, what are my options? She listed them in her head: leave the area or get the photographer.

The last one sounded like the best use of time and opportunity. That camera contained too much information to give it up now. She might never work again if this got out. It would be best to move now, with no more delays. She didn't know for sure that the photographer was still there. Standing here was stupid, she decided. But there was one thing to do first. She should call her employer and see if they could find out who the photographer was. The problem here was that the evidence might then end up in their hands. But did it really matter? They were ruining her life enough already.

Keeping the garage in sight, she dialed a number.

"I need some information - - Where I am is not important - - Are you on-site yet? - - You are? Good. There was a third party on the target roof. She is a witness - - You knew that? Oh, the security in the helicopter. Of course. I need to know who she is - - Yes, I will take care of her for us. No charge - - Okay, call me immediately."

She didn't mention the camera. Some things you keep to yourself.

**

"Hello - - Where are you? - - Yes - - We know - - I think we can help each other - - That is acceptable, I'll call when I have the information."

Ryu DaeHo returned the phone to his pocket and turned to the two building guards standing, as ordered, with their backs to the wall. They were in a room immediately behind the security desk in the lobby of the building. A desk held two computer monitors, each displaying six views of different areas inside the building. An NIS agent was sitting at the desk and fast-forwarding through video from the last four hours. He reached out to the keyboard and pressed a key, freezing the action. Another key-press filled the screen with the view he was interested in.

"Here it is," he announced without turning round.

Ryu DaeHo leaned forward and peered at the screen as the agent played the video at regular speed. He saw one of the guards accepting an envelope, and a stuffed animal, and then escorting a girl through a delivery entrance.

"Is this someone's girlfriend?" he asked the room in general.

There was no response.

"Well?"

He turned back to the guard whose image was on the screen.

"You allowed someone to enter the building and apparently accepted a bribe. Let me spell this out for you. Two of our agents died and you almost certainly allowed someone on to the roof, yes?"

The guard nodded reluctantly.

"Do you expect me, or a court if we bother with one, to believe that the two are not linked?"

The guard glanced at the stuffed animal on the table, and thought of his daughter.

Ryu DaeHo followed his gaze. "I want to know who she is. If you tell me quickly, it will be better for you. Do you want to see your child again?"

"She works for a private detective. She just wanted to observe a meeting in the hotel." He looked toward the other guard. "We had no idea that a helicopter was scheduled to land here tonight until just before it arrived. Anyway, they would never do this kind of thing. They gave me money to buy a meal on the way home. That's all. And he used to be one of you..."

"Who?"

"Jung RaeWon. The girl works for him, she is new."

"Jung RaeWon! Are you sure?" His mind started spinning with this new information. First he was forced to deal with that woman a few weeks ago, and now another ex-agent had popped up. Now he remembered that they had left the NIS at about the same time. What was their connection? Was there a connection? Coincidence? Were they working together? Did they know what was going on? Why else would they be at the same location as the contractor? How did they know?

He felt as though his head was going to explode. His ability to take in this data and make sense of it was being severely tested. He needed some fresh air.

"I'll be back in a minute. Get a copy of her picture back to headquarters. Copy the video and delete the original."

The agent at the desk nodded, but knew better than to say anything.

What else could go wrong, Ryu DaeHo wondered. Oh well, at least no one had fallen off the roof.

***

The traffic slowed enough for the assassin to run across the five lanes of vehicles to the center. Five more to go. She angled a little more to the south, hoping that the photographer, if she was still there, wouldn't expect her from that direction. She made it across, despite nearly being impaled by a motorcycle, and staying close to the buildings, walking slowly north.

With the parking garage in sight, she reached inside her jacket and removed the pistol from the holster. Shielding it from view, she felt in a pocket for a silencer and attached it to the gun.

Making sure that the safety was off and a round was in the chamber, she held the weapon hidden from sight.

Perhaps the photographer was a rookie, why she hadn't kept moving? All the better for me, she thought. There she was, hard to see unless you knew what you were looking for. Or perhaps desperation had improved her eyesight. As she watched, the photographer stood up and moved further in to the garage. This was her opportunity. The target moved out of her line of sight. The shooter moved to the low railing behind a line of phone boxes and climbed over, constantly scanning for her target. She saw her, walking quickly away, but not in cover.

Any other people around? No. She raised the gun and squeezed off two rounds at the back of the photographer.

Chapter Twelve

June 03 | 19:30

On the street outside his office RaeWon finished dialing Sora and put the phone to his ear.

"Sora, you have to keep moving. You're very close to Namdaemun market, so go one street east and then south. Go down in to the underground arcade, buy something to change your appearance, then get out as soon as possible on the other side of the road. Meet me at Gate Eight on the west side of the market. I'll be there in twenty minutes."

He stopped a taxi and got in.

***

Sora knew that RaeWon was right and that the best idea was to keep moving. Moving and turning. She now knew what a real situation could do to a mind. If she had been playing the 'game', she would never have moved in a straight line and gone to ground like she had tonight. She jabbed a finger against her head and admonished herself that she needed to be alert if she wanted to see tomorrow.

She stood and started moving deeper in to the garage. The

stress was beginning to make her feel tired, the backpack feeling heavier with every passing minute. Realizing that she was walking out in the open she moved to the left to get between cars. She felt something whistle past her and heard two impacts as something hit a metal roof support.

That woke her up. The sound was familiar from the roof. She ducked between two cars and kept moving, jumping over a low barrier and almost hitting several people walking by in the alleyway. She turned to her right and ran, dodging between groups of people, not caring about the looks they gave her.

***

Back at the scene of the assassination, Ryu DaeHo called his office.

"I want men sent to the homes and workplaces of Park YeJin and Jung RaeWon. They are to be detained for questioning about the shooting of our agents tonight - - They also have a younger female accomplice, bring her in as well. A photograph of the girl is on its way."

Orders issued, he made a second call to the contract assassin.

"I know who she is, or rather I know who she works for - - An ex-NIS agent, Jung RaeWon - - I've sent men to find him. Do you know where the girl is now? - - You missed? - - Okay, I'll send some men to that area. I don't want you leaving more dead bodies on the streets - - We'll be in touch. You should consider going to ground for a while, before the next phase."

***

The shooter ran after the photographer, gun held ready in front of her. She lowered it as she saw the people in the alleyway. She was aware of the photographer running to the east. Her phone vibrated.

"Yes," she said and heard the irritation in her own voice, " - - Who? - - If you know who he is, take care of him, he's an untidy detail, one of several - - She was just in a parking garage a couple of blocks to the south. I fired at her but she got away - - Yes, I missed. She seems to have the luck of the devil - - But if I see her first I'm going to take her out."

Chapter Thirteen

June 03 | 19:45

Sora wasn't sure that she liked RaeWon's idea about descending underground. However she thought about it, she couldn't get the image of trapping herself out of her mind. But, she reminded herself, he is the expert. And she hadn't forgotten the lesson of a few minutes ago: keep moving and turning.

So she forced herself down the stairs and in to the arcade. She looked around as she walked, knowing exactly what she needed to do. She was dressed all in black, carrying a black backpack, and that needed to change. Ten minutes later, she had purchased two windbreakers, of different colors, and two matching ball caps. Before she left the arcade, she replaced her black jacket with a light blue one, and put the old jacket in the backpack.

On her way to one of the south exits, she found a multicolored scarf, which when tied on to the backpack made it look decidedly less black.

Satisfied that she looked different from before, even if not completely fashionable, she started up the stairs, and kept walking when she reached the street. A quick turn took her in to the Namdaemun market streets. Making her way through the people, she found her next turn, a sign pointing to the police station.

Gate Eight appeared ahead of her and at the street, she exited the market and turned left to head south, looking for a place to wait without being too conspicuous. Once she reached Gate Seven, she crossed the street to the west side and took-up position near a food vendor. Despite the wonderful smells from the food, she was too nervous to eat.

From here, traffic permitting, she had a reasonable view of the two gates across the street and she didn't feel as though she was just standing and waiting with a neon sign attached to her back. The view was a compromise of being in cover versus being able to see everything. She felt confident that she would see RaeWon when he arrived and could cross the street fairly quickly.

Sora was starting to feel more awake and the fatigue was drifting away, bit by bit. She felt more focused than she had for a while and her confidence was returning. If people were going to try and kill her, the least she could do was be an active participant rather than a sitting duck. Her uncle had been right, life was dangerous.

***

Park YeJin had spent the afternoon editing some photographs from a portrait session and generally organizing images. Tired from sitting in front of the computer for so long, she leaned back in the chair and stretched. She glanced at the time: 19:20. That was enough, she decided, time for a drink and perhaps something to eat.

As she was thinking about what to eat, the phone rang.

" - - Yes, everything okay? - - What! Is she hurt? - - What? - - Tell me - - "

She listened as RaeWon briefly described what Sora was going though.

"A photo? Of course. Look, we have to help her."

With RaeWon's assurance that he was on his way to help, the call ended. YeJin waited for the photo to arrive from Sora, pacing around, the second hand on the clock barely moving.

A few minutes later, the message arrived in her email. Opening the attachment, the image of a pretty woman reaching out for a cap was on the screen. She stared at it in amazement. YeJin recognized the woman instantly. How could it be the same person, though? What kind of coincidence was this? They had to help Sora, YeJin was sure of that.

She called RaeWon, her hand starting to shake as the ramifications of this information ran through her head.

"RaeWon, what are we going to do? I don't know what this means! - - We need to know - - Yes, and we know who it is - - the job I did for the NIS, it's the same woman - - Yes, of course I'm sure - -" The line went dead.

YeJin sat and stared at the picture, beginning to calm down. She had never been a field agent and any mission she was involved in was usually taking place overseas. While she cared about the agents she worked with, it had been somehow like a game. This was all too real. And Sora was in the middle of it.

The phone rang again.

"Hello - - Where? - - When? - - Payment? - - Yes - - On the west of the market, yes - - "

She waited while RaeWon paused. It seemed like he wanted to say something, but didn't know what or how to say it. He settled for urging her to hurry, then ended the call.

Heeding his urging, she hurried to Sora's room and found her passport, which she would need to make the reservations. Then, at the computer she started to make the travel arrangements he had requested. It didn't take long as they didn't intend to use them; YeJin selected random flights over the next couple of days. Being careful of RaeWon's money, she bought tickets which could be refunded.

Task completed, she took a backpack from the storage room and dropped the passports inside. A laptop, power supply, and cables followed. An external drive containing data she didn't want to lose was next. From her small safe she took whatever cash was there. Grabbing a jacket, she was ready to go. She stood in the kitchen and looked around, unable to shake a sudden feeling that she would be away for a while. Some fruit caught her eye and that went into the backpack as well, followed by some bottled water.

One last thing to do, she pulled the hard drive from the front of the computer case, then opened the case and removed the memory chips. These were the last things in to the backpack.

Remembering RaeWon's warning to get out fast, she left the building and locked the door behind her.

As she walked down the lane to the road, she worried about Sora. YeJin had never been shot at and she was sure that this was a first for Sora, too. If they hadn't got her yet, she would be okay, right?

At the road, she stopped a taxi and left for the market.

***

The two NIS agents were driving, in no particular hurry, to Park YeJin's studio. Another team were on their way to her home. They did not know if she would be at the studio, and didn't actually think she would be, but orders were orders.

The passenger pointed to the side of the road.

"It's up this lane, drop me here and I'll walk up there. Wait for me." He glanced at her photograph again. "She's pretty. Used to be one of us, huh."

He got out of the car and walked toward the lane. As he did, he saw YeJin getting in to a taxi. He was too far away to stop her, so he quickly returned to the car.

"Follow that taxi, she's inside."

"Should I stop the taxi?" asked the driver.

"No, let's follow and see if she meets up with this other girl they wanted."

The driver drove silently as his partner looked again at the pictures of the two women.

"Actually, they're both pretty. They don't seem dangerous to me."

***

Jung RaeWon had the taxi drop him at the Namsan Stairs. While he waited for it to leave he quietly scanned the area for suspicious people or vehicles which were already there or which might have followed him. The few people that were around seemed to be concentrating on a couple recreating a scene from a drama which had made the Stairs so famous. Cute, but not suspicious.

A message arrived from YeJin saying that she was on her way.

Satisfied that he didn't have anyone tailing him, he turned north and started walking toward the market. He knew it would take him about ten minutes and he hurried so that Sora would not have to be on her own for longer than absolutely necessary.

Another message, this time from Sora. She was in position, and obviously still alive.

He carefully scanned as he went, more alert than he had been for what now seemed like a very long time. He felt the old feelings from his days as an agent returning. It felt good, he had missed that time more than he had realized.

He was making good progress as he headed down the hill, walking on the right of the road. As he went he looked for stairs to descend to the streets below him. Just before the next bend of the road, he found a way. When he reached the bottom, he started jogging toward Namdaemun market. Soon he could see the street which bordered the south side of the market.

He was about fifty meters from the junction when he saw a black vehicle pull to the side of the road and park as if it owned the street. He could clearly see the shapes of four men inside. His gut told him this was not good. They were facing away from him, as though watching the market exit. He saw their bodies making small movements which he knew meant they were checking their weapons. This was an NIS team. He had done this enough times himself to know the signs.

He kept walking, rounded the corner and entered a mart. As he browsed their drinks he tried to work out what their presence meant. He knew that Sora was not near this entrance and that YeJin was heading toward Sora. And that neither had plans to move in to the market. So, they must have information that Sora had moved in this direction, but not about where she was. And if one team was at this entrance, was there a team at each entrance? That was a lot of man-power.

RaeWon had planned to go through the market to meet with Sora. That might not be the best idea, he thought.

Leaving the mart, he collided with a man. He caught sight of a radio ear-piece and muttering an apology tried to walk away, but the man turned in surprise and called after him.

"Jung RaeWon-shi!"

He had been recognized. RaeWon turned back toward the man, smiled and greeted him like a long-lost friend. People on the street lost interest in what looked like it could have an interesting event. RaeWon moved closer and extended his arms to hug the man, pushing him behind a vendors kiosk and against a large, metal street sign support. As he did, RaeWon struck him with his forehead on the nose. The man wobbled on his feet for a moment and RaeWon pushed him down to the ground, ramming the back of the agents head against the metal pole. The man was unconscious but RaeWon talked to him as though he was an old friend who needed help. People kept moving and ignored them.

As he continued to talk to him, RaeWon went though his pockets. Putting the backpack next to him, a gun, wallet, and the radio went inside. RaeWon flicked open the identification and confirmed that he was with the NIS.

How much worse could things get?

He had to collect the girls and get out of town. Sora was only 300 meters away and YeJin would be here soon if she wasn't already. He hoisted the pack on his back, left the unfortunate agent sitting on the ground, and walked away. He found a darkened doorway and stopped to send a message to Sora.

Hold position. NIS here.

A moment later the response arrived.

Too late.

Chapter Fourteen

Sora shifted her weight from one foot to the other as she stood in a dark doorway, across the road from the market. She swept the area between the two entrances to the market with her eyes. Which direction would YeJin arrive from? Probably the south, she thought. She scanned the road, back and forth, phone to her ear pretending to be making a phone call.

A message arrived. It was from Jung RaeWon.

Hold position. NIS here.

At almost the same time, a bus passed and as her view cleared she saw YeJin approaching from her right on the other side of the street. She was almost at Gate Seven. Sora looked back in the direction YeJin had arrived from and spotted a car pull in behind a taxi and a man jump out from the passenger seat. The man moved quickly, hurrying to get round a crowd of people. He could not have stood out more if he had tried. Instinctively, Sora was already moving from her doorway and merged with the people crossing the road as she sent a reply.

Too late.

When she was half way across, the man was about ten meters behind YeJin. When Sora reached the market side of the road, she waited for YeJin to pass the fruit vendors, walked directly toward her and said, "Keep moving."

YeJin was surprised, but kept walking. Sora turned abruptly to her right and stood waiting for the man. Too late he saw her standing in his path and suddenly realized who she was. He decided he was outnumbered and started to reach inside his jacket, but his hand did not make it to his gun.

At the same moment that he made a promise to himself never to underestimate pretty girls, Sora's foot connected with the side of his head. He lost the ability to concentrate on anything other than the pain and barely felt his legs as they were swept away beneath him and he hit the ground.

Sora ran to YeJin and grabbed her arm. "He has a partner, let's get off the street and out of sight."

Pulling YeJin behind her, Sora led the way up some steps and in to a multi-story store. Inside they zigged and zagged until they found some stairs, then ran up them and tried to make themselves invisible amongst the people. Sora took off her jacket and stayed near the top of the stairs, ready to send anyone that followed back to the bottom.

YeJin took a bundle out of her pack and handed it to Sora.

"This is your passport and some cash, in case we get separated. Do you have a spare battery for your phone?"

Sora nodded. "Yes, but let's try to stay together, okay?"

It was YeJin's turn to nod.

Sora felt as though she was running completely on adrenaline. Was this what fifty cups of coffee felt like?

Time to call for help.

"RaeWon - - I stopped a man who was following YeJin and we're hiding in a building next to Gate Seven - - Yes, I'm at the top of some stairs - - There was another agent in a car, just south of here - - we'll be ready."

***

Too late.

Jung RaeWon started moving a little faster. He wanted to get there quickly, but he didn't want to run in to any more NIS agents if he could avoid it. And he couldn't be certain where Sora was now.

A call arrived from Sora.

"Yes - - inside? - - top of the stairs, okay. Was anyone with him? - - Stay where you are, I'll be there in two minutes. I'll make sure the area is clean outside, and then you can come out and we'll leave the area. Be ready."

Nearing the area around Gate Seven his scan spotted a black car abandoned at the edge of the road. He remembered the radio. Fishing it out of his pack, he inserted the ear-piece and adjusted the volume.

"...they went in to a store next to Gate Seven. My partner is down, but he'll be okay. This girl is dangerous."

RaeWon smiled proudly.

"Wait outside and make sure they don't get past you if they try to leave. Use any force necessary."

His smile disappeared as he recognized the last voice as Ryu DaeHo. He looked around for the agent. There he was, at the bottom of the steps helping his partner to his feet. He dialed Sora.

"Sora, I'm outside. There are two agents here and they have been authorized to use force, so be very careful. Are you both okay? - - Start making your way downstairs. I don't think any agents are inside with you, come to the door where you came in. Stay on the line and let me know when you are in position."

He looked over at the men, one standing with his gun drawn, the other rubbing his head. Sora told him they were ready.

"Count to ten slowly and come out, make your way to their car. Go."

Checking his own gun, he counted down slowly. When he saw Sora and YeJin appear in the doorway, he started moving through the vendors toward the agents.

The agents saw the girls at the same time and one raised his gun, while the other pulled his weapon from inside his jacket. The agents shouted commands at them. People saw the guns and started scattering. Soon the immediate area was deserted. RaeWon continued moving, gun at the ready, while their attention was distracted.

"Raise your hands. Now!" he shouted at the agents.

Confused, they began to turn.

"Hands up!" he commanded.

When they saw his gun, one of them decided that RaeWon was close enough that he was unlikely to miss and raised his hands. The other, still annoyed that Sora had taken him down, continued to move his gun toward RaeWon. RaeWon shot him in the leg before the gun was on him and moved his aim back to the other agent.

While the first agent was on the ground for the second time that day, RaeWon motioned the other man away from his partner and walked over to put his foot on the gun still in the hand of the agent writhing on the ground in front of him.

"Turn around," he instructed. "Don't be brave. Your partner will be okay and so will you, so turn around."

The agent turned. RaeWon scooped up the gun from the ground and beckoned for the girls to come over. He handed the gun to Sora, then took the gun from the other agent.

"Please don't point that at anyone," he told Sora, who looked at the gun and nodded.

"On your knees," he told the agent, then, "On your face and give me your radio. Slowly."

YeJin took the radio from the wounded man and turned it off. RaeWon did the same with the other. Both radios went in to a backpack.

Kicking the agent gently in the ribs to get his attention, "Look after your partner. I don't know what they told you about us, but we haven't done anything wrong."

RaeWon nodded in the direction of the car, still sitting with its doors open and engine running. They all turned to leave.

And at that moment their simple plan went off the rails.

Chapter Fifteen

Two NIS agents appeared as if from nowhere at the top of the steps, guns in front of them.

"Stop, Police!" they called.

RaeWon groaned to himself, well aware that the sight of the agents lying on the ground was not going to make them any friends. Sora, a few steps ahead, moved in to cover behind a vendors food cart.

YeJin and RaeWon turned and put their hands in the air. YeJin looked at RaeWon, but he didn't take his eyes off the men now moving toward their colleagues on the ground. And they didn't take their eyes off him either.

"Stand very still," he whispered to YeJin.

There was now about six meters between them and the agents. RaeWon had his gun on the finger of one hand raised in the air and the radio in his ear.

"*What's happening? Report.*" Ryu DaeHo's irritating voice again. Even in the dark RaeWon could tell that these agents were not enjoying having to answer to him. It was something about their body language.

One of the agents spoke in to his microphone. "One agent shot. We need medical assistance. We have the suspects."

"*Cuckoo, are you in position?*"

"Cuckoo will be landing in ten."

Another agent on the way, wondered RaeWon.

One of the agents, who had not moved his gun or his eyes from RaeWon, spoke, "Put the gun on the ground."

RaeWon started to slowly lower his gun toward the concrete at his feet. Arms pointing out from each side of his body horizontally, the gun was half way to the ground when to the surprise of everyone a warning was shouted from an agent running down the steps from the store.

"Gun. He has a gun!"

For a split second there was total confusion. Everyone froze in position, momentarily distracted by the newcomer. One second the situation seemed to be under control and the next nobody was quite sure where the danger was. But the man rushing forward seemed to know and he fired two quick shots as he ran.

The bullets missed RaeWon, who raised his own gun and fired two shots in return. The agent fell, rolling down the remaining steps. The agents understood this new threat and fired at RaeWon who wasn't where they expected him to be as he rolled away from his former position. He returned fire, hitting one agent in the throat and the second in the chest. The third didn't have a weapon and retreated against a wall.

The threat neutralized for the moment, RaeWon turned to grab YeJin's arm, but she wasn't there. He looked from left to right, then nearly tripped over her. She was lying on the ground. Time seemed to stop for RaeWon. Remembering that you can't protect someone if you're dead, he resumed his scan of the scene. The unarmed agent was running away to the north in the direction of Gate Eight. They had to get out of there. Now. There was a police station at Gate Eight and somebody must have raised an alarm by now. Although with the NIS on site they may have been told to stand down.

He hurried over to YeJin.

"Sora, help me," he called over his shoulder.

Bending down he checked for a pulse. It was there, but weak. He could see that she had been hit in the side.

Looking at the street he saw a delivery vehicle parked with it's rear gate open.

"Sora, check if there are keys in that truck."

Sora ran over and looked through the window.

"Yes," she called.

"Help me get YeJin in the back."

Together they lifted YeJin and carried her to the truck, placing her in the back as gently as possible.

"No time for first aid," said RaeWon. "We have to leave and get her some help."

He reached for Sora's gun.

"This is how you hold it," he said, demonstrating. "This ejects the magazine." He ejected it and examined the contents. It was full. "You have seventeen rounds." He replaced the magazine and handed the gun back to her. "Point. Shoot. Here is a spare magazine. Let's go."

He shut the rear of the truck and went round to the drivers door. Before he could open it, a hail of bullets struck the truck and the ground in front of it. He raised his gun and saw three armed men approaching from the direction of Gate Eight. He returned fire and the men took cover.

RaeWon continued to get in to the truck and started the engine. The men reappeared and he heard shots from Sora. Looking through the passenger window, he saw Sora standing, gun in hand. She fired another shot.

"Go!" she yelled. "Go. I'll call you."

She fired again, keeping the men out of sight, moving herself away from the truck.

"Get in! Sora!"

She ignored him. He had a split-second to make a decision and he made one. He reversed the truck in to the street and drove off, away from the men ... and Sora. He heard more shots and in the mirror thought he saw Sora running in to the market.

He punched the steering wheel in frustration. This was not how the plan was supposed to go.

CHAPTER SIXTEEN

Sora saw the men approaching, firing as they ran. Almost without thinking, she pointed her gun in their direction and squeezed the trigger. One round just to get the feel, then another three. She was surprised at how clinically she was thinking. Perhaps RaeWon was having a calming effect on her after she had watched his cool actions under duress. The men stopped shooting and retreated in to cover. She fired another shot in their direction for good measure.

She was conscious of RaeWon yelling for her to get in the truck.

But wouldn't that leave them too exposed to make their escape? They should leave without her, she thought. She was scared, but didn't it make more sense to divide the people chasing them?

"Go!" she yelled. "Go. I'll call you. Help YeJin."

She moved away from the truck to help RaeWon make his decision, firing to keep the men in cover more than having any hope of hitting anything. The truck backed in to the street and accelerated away to the south, leaving her behind.

The men were firing after the truck. Firing back at them, she ran out of their line of sight, under Gate Seven and in to the market. Soon she was among people, but she kept moving until she felt that she was among people that didn't know what had been going on. The gun was now hidden in her jacket pocket.

Turn, she remembered, keep turning. Don't move in a straight line.

This was easier to say than to do. She wanted to put distance between her and any guns that might be following. Should she go to ground now and hope that they would run past her? No, better to have more distance so that the size of their search area would be increased.

Sora had slowed to a fast walk, blending in with the people.

Almost immediately it was time to make another decision as she reached the first intersection. Left, right, or continue on? To her right she could see the top of a bus over the heads of the crowd as it drove by what must obviously be a way out. Left would take her north and away from the immediate exit and deeper in to the market. If she did neither she would have to make the same decision very soon at another junction.

Sora remembered that RaeWon had seen NIS agents at the south of the market. She decided that she'd had enough of feeling like she was trapped in a box and turned to the right toward the way out.

Just before she got to the road she carefully surveyed the street ahead. Surely if they were nearby and they had been told which way she had run, they would be watching the exit? Sora couldn't see anyone that looked like a threat. She was filled with an overwhelming desire to get out of the area. Not a panic, just a strong desire.

But then, to her left, she saw two men moving in her direction. They were still a couple of hundred meters away, but they looked like they were on a mission rather than just looking for a good deal on pork.

A motorcycle pulled in to the side of the road directly in front of her, a delivery box fastened to the rear. A boy jumped off and dropped his helmet on the seat. Moving to the box, he unfastened the lid and pulled out a large envelope. He let the lid drop back in to place and jogging past her, entered a store. Sora did not need to be told that this was a golden opportunity and moved immediately. When she had some vendor kiosks between her and the agents, she quickened her pace, making sure the pack was secure on her back. Grabbing the helmet and slipping her head inside, she put the bike in first gear and accelerated away down the bus lane, merging with the main flow at the first opportunity. Sora was no stranger to riding on two wheels and she threaded her way through the cars and trucks, paying close attention to any buses that got too close.

Amazingly, even though she had just stolen a vehicle, she felt like a weight had been lifted from her shoulders.

But what would RaeWon do now? What would her uncle expect her to do? And how was YeJin? Some of the weight came back.

Sora was sure that the owner would immediately report the theft and the agents might have seen her leave. So she needed to park it and walk, or take side roads. Taking the first turn to the left, she rode south and continued to skirt Namsan Park.

A little over five minutes later, she reached the Yongsan Ga-Dong area and turned in to the maze of smaller streets. Trying to continue south, she looked for a suitable place to hide the bike. Just before the buildings became more residential an opportunity presented itself on an empty street. A pile of building materials that looked like it had not been disturbed for a long time. The bike went behind a large piece of dry-wall and was covered with a discarded piece of paint-covered canvas.

Sora knew that she hadn't put a lot of distance between her and the market, perhaps only a couple of kilometers, but that would increase their search area a lot. With no plan, she was reluctant to go too far in any one direction just in case RaeWon wanted her to go somewhere specific. Grabbing the pack, she walked away and didn't look back. Where could she hide?

It was time to contact RaeWon.

***

RaeWon drove like a mad-man for ten minutes, desperate to get out of the market area. To get out of the area was logical, but it also seemed as though getting away from the scene of the shooting would heal YeJin. He recognized this thought as ridiculous and forced himself to calm down. This was why he had always preferred to work alone in the field and certainly never with a woman he had feelings for. And finally admitting those feelings jerked him back to reality.

His goal was to find medical attention for YeJin. He had an idea who might help him, but he needed to change vehicles first. Too many people had seen this one. He found his mind wandering again. Having a precious cargo definitely messed with your mind, he realized. He forced himself to think about what balance to put on distance from the agents versus changing vehicles versus finding a doctor.

The more he drove away from the market area, the less cameras there were to track him. Cameras! Yes, he needed to find a car park outside the city center zone where he could find another car. A few more minutes should do it.

He had a rudimentary knowledge of first aid from his field training with the NIS. There was always the chance of an agent being injured on a mission, but being able to walk in to a hospital was a luxury you almost never had. This was one of those occasions, only this time he was on home ground and not struggling to survive in a hostile environment. He grinned wryly. Actually there was no difference in this case. No chance of going to a hospital and everyone and everything was not only hostile, but getting more hostile by the minute as word spread about the incident.

Could he leave her at a hospital? He could, but a gun shot wound would be reported and acted on almost immediately, putting YeJin in the custody of the NIS where she could be ... what? What would they do? Interrogate her? About what? Well, the NIS knew that the three of them knew each other and were potentially acting together. And they had left least several dead agents behind them.

They could use her as a bargaining piece against Sora and himself. They could make her take the fall for the shooting. And what about the fake documents she had made for them? How did those figure in to the situation?

What was he thinking? He wasn't about to leave her anywhere, ever. After he made this decision he found he was much calmer.

The traffic had not been too heavy, allowing him to make good time. Now that he was out of the immediate danger area he felt more comfortable tending to YeJin's wound. He pulled over to the side of the road and left the engine running. He turned and leaned in to the rear where YeJin lay quietly. Placing two fingers on her neck to check her pulse, he found it, but it wasn't as strong as he would have liked.

Reaching for the backpack on the passenger seat next to him, he brought out a medical kit. He opened it and quickly pulled on a pair of gloves. Next he found two field dressings and placed them on top of YeJin's still form. He took out a knife and cut away her blood-soaked clothing around the wound area. The bullet had entered from the front, just above the hip, and reaching underneath her he found an exit wound at the back. What he couldn't tell, of course, was what damage had been done on it's way through.

He applied the dressings to the wound, one to the front and one to the back, rolling her body enough to allow access. He secured them with tape. Looking at the floor of the truck, he hoped that the blood loss was less than it looked. He needed to find help. He discard the gloves next to her still form.

As he held his phone in one hand and checked the mirrors for anyone paying too much attention, he wondered who would be the best person to call. Who did he know that could be trusted not to call the authorities or ask too many questions?

He checked his watch. Time to move, he had been stationary for too long. He decided to find somewhere discrete to park the vehicle so that he could plan his next moves.

He pulled out in to the traffic aware that the huge letters on the side of the truck were an invitation for him to be spotted. He took the first turn to the right and left the busier road for a quieter, but narrower, street and drove alongside the Hyochang soccer stadium. Out of the corner of his eye, he saw two trucks parking down a side road. He stopped and reversed back a few meters. The drivers had parked and were leaving their vehicles, carrying their jackets and lunch bags. They laughed as the walked away, obviously happy that the day was over and perhaps looking forward to some beer and chicken.

When they had disappeared from sight, RaeWon turned toward their parked trucks and found exactly what he was hoping for; a space between two vehicles where he could stop and not have the name on his truck advertise his position. After he put the truck in the welcoming space, he turned off the engine and enjoyed the silence for a moment. It was broken by YeJin moaning gently behind him. Turning to her again, he wiped some beads of sweat from her forehead. He was worried that she would wake soon and begin to feel the pain. The medical kit still lay beside him and taking a syringe, he injected some morphine in to her arm.

He knew he couldn't drive around all night with a gun-shot victim, but who could he call? He found it a little funny that if he was overseas he would have a list of people he could call. But here, in his own back-yard, it would be much harder to get help.

He grabbed the phone and dialed a number.

"*Hello?*" The voice was of someone older. A man.

"I have an emergency and I need help."

"*Are you injured?*"

"No, but my friend is. Gunshot."

There was a sharp intake of breath from the other end of the line. The voice belonged to the man he and Sora had taken the USB drive to for investigation.

"I need a doctor. Can you recommend?"

"*Is it --?*"

"YeJin. Can you help?"

"*Of course. Wait.*" There was a pause and RaeWon looked for the pen in his pack and wrote down the number. "*Tell her the code is octopus.*"

"Thank you. I'll be in touch." RaeWon ended the call. He immediately dialed the number.

"*Yes?*" A woman's voice. She didn't sound young or old.

"I need medical assistance for a friend. Can you help?"

"*The code?*"

"Octopus."

"*I understand. What will I be treating?*"

"Gunshot, right side. Female, early thirties, condition stable. Where will we meet?"

The voice gave an address and some landmarks, which he wrote down. "*Park underneath.*"

"I'm on my way."

***

The address was about four kilometers south west of his current location, on the other side of the Han River.

Should he risk staying with the truck or should he find another vehicle? He decided that as he wasn't having to go back toward the danger area, he would skip finding and transferring YeJin to another vehicle, and just leave.

The engine started and he pulled out of the parking spot. YeJin remained quiet and he was glad that she didn't seem to be feeling any pain at the moment. A few minutes later he was back amongst the traffic and then on a bridge heading south over the Han. Once on the other side he drove steadily away from the water and looked for the first landmark indicating he should turn.

As he left the main road, he continued watching his mirrors for unwelcome attention, but didn't see any. Two more turns brought him to his destination. He saw the entrance to the garage and slowed. Once inside he headed for the back, away from the entrance and looked for a spot near the elevator. As he turned the engine off, there was a knock on the passenger window. RaeWon had the gun trained on the source of the sound in a milli-second, startling the young man standing there.

"Octopus," said the man, who seemed to be in his early twenties, and had wisely kept his hands in sight to show they were empty.

RaeWon lowered the gun, gathered his pack, and got out without taking his eyes from their new friend.

They both went to the rear of the truck and RaeWon opened the doors.

"Help me get her out," he said.

Despite his young age, the guy helped RaeWon without seeming to be shocked about the blood on the floor of the truck. YeJin moaned as they handled her and together they carried her to the nearby freight elevator. As they entered, RaeWon noted that the floor had been covered with material to catch any blood. He approved of the preparation, it was a good sign about the way this doctor conducted business.

They went up to the third floor, the top one, and exited the elevator. Again there was material on the floor leading to a doorway which was opened as they approached. A woman was waiting. Without a word she assisted them in getting YeJin in to an examination room and on to a table.

Now the woman spoke. "Our mutual friend called me and told me to take good care of you both. He seems to be very fond of the lady. And you, too. He said that if she did not survive for your wedding there would be big trouble." She smiled. "You can trust us. He will explain when you see him next time."

RaeWon grunted, still concerned about YeJin.

"Did you leave anything in the truck?"

RaeWon shook his head and the woman turned to the man who was leaving. "Gather the materials, put them in the truck and drive it away from here. Abandon it --"

"I know, I know. I'll take care of it, don't worry." He lifted a hand in goodbye and left.

As the door closed behind him, the woman locked it. She returned to the room and washed her hands. Pulling on a pair of gloves, she removed the dressings and began to methodically inspect the wound, gently rolling YeJin on to her side to check the exit. Next, she slowly pushed a finger in to the hole made by the bullet and probed inside, causing YeJin to moan again.

She withdrew and turned to RaeWon. "The bullet went though. I don't see or feel any obvious damage to bone or organs. I'll take a closer look and then close the wound. When that is done, my colleague will return with another vehicle and you can take her away. Any questions?"

RaeWon shook his head. "No, and thank you. If you don't need me for a minute, I have a call to make."

The doctor gestured dismissively and he left YeJin in her hands to search for his phone. It was time to check on Sora. He left the room and found their packs where he had left them as they came in.

Dialing the number, he listened as the phone rang. It was answered after the first ring. But he didn't recognize the voice.

***

As she walked away, leaving the motorbike hidden behind her, Sora was satisfied that it would not be quickly discovered. She looked around for somewhere to hide as she walked. It didn't have to be perfect, she thought, just good enough for a short while until she could talk with RaeWon.

After five minutes she found a possible spot. Looking around without looking as though she was checking for a tail, she crossed a small parking area and moved toward a set of stairs which looked like they would provide a dark space to hide in. A large cardboard box sat, abandoned, under the stairs and she decided that it would make a good temporary shelter. Some other boxes had been broken down and stored inside her new house and those became somewhere to sit, providing some small distance between her and the cold ground.

Once settled inside, the phone came out and she stared at it. Should she call now, or wait, she wondered. After the noise of the market and then the motorbike, the silence seemed to be closing in on her. Without realizing, she dozed off where she sat. She was brought back to consciousness by her phone vibrating. She rubbed an eye and tried to focus on the screen.

"Hello?" Sora suddenly realized that she was alone. She knew she was on her own, but the prospect of hearing RaeWon's voice was a reminder that he wasn't there to help her and that YeJin had been shot. "RaeWon, are you okay? How is YeJin?"

RaeWon's voice came back, reassuringly steady. "*The doctor is looking at her now and she is going to be okay. I didn't recognize your voice, are you safe at the moment?"*

"Yes, I'm safe. But I'm a little scared. What do I do now? Am I going to have to run for the rest of my life? I don't know how long I can do this for --."

"Calm down, Sora, take a breath. Truthfully, I don't know how long this will go on for, but we'll survive. I'm going to have to find a place to hide with YeJin so that she can recover. So we won't be moving around too much. I'm going to find somewhere for you to go, but we won't be able to meet up for a little while. I have an idea, but let me finish the arrangements and I'll get back to you with the plan. Do you have the documents and money that YeJin brought for you?"

"Yes."

"Can you stay where you are for a few more hours?"

"Yes. I'm --"

"Don't tell me over an open line. If you can stay where you are for another hour, I'll call you back. Can you do that?"

"Yes."

"Understood. I will call you in one hour or less. Be ready."

The call ended and Sora felt a little better after her momentary panic attack. Be ready? What else did he think she would be doing?

She truly thought that the only reason she was still free was because of luck. But how long could it last? She wasn't a pro like them. Her panic was over for the moment, but tiredness was coming over her again. She checked the time and decided that if she hadn't heard from RaeWon within the hour as he promised, she would do something on her own. But what? Sora wasn't scared of being on her own in the world, just of being on her own against people who actually wanted to do her harm. Sitting in the dark under the stairs, it seemed as though they might pursue her for the rest of her life.

She would have to get out of town, she decided. Busan, perhaps? Yes! She could retrieve the motorbike and spray it a different color and remove the big delivery box on the back. And change the license plate. How long would all that take? And could she do it without anyone seeing and being suspicious?

Sora lay down and pulled some of the cardboard over herself. With one of the jackets under her head and clutching the pack to her stomach, she was asleep in thirty seconds.

Chapter Seventeen

RaeWon glanced back toward the room where the doctor was bent over YeJin's body. He wondered why, as much as he liked YeJin, that he wasn't more panicked about her condition. Did he like her less than he had thought? Was he just a cold-hearted bastard who didn't deserve her? Perhaps.

Then he recognized the scenario. He was protecting himself, covering himself in an icy, impenetrable layer that personal feelings could not get though. This reminded him, again, of his days in the field with the NIS, working in foreign countries with people trying to stop him. Those days were long gone and he had no desire to relive them. If he thought about all the killing and subterfuge for too long, he started to dislike the man he was. Or had been. Was he really that different now? He certainly hadn't hesitated to shoot the men back at the market and that had come very naturally. Obviously his past was not too far beneath the surface.

But that had been to protect the girls. Protect? That was a joke. One was shot and the other was hiding goodness knows where, probably frightened out of her mind. What could he do for them? For them all?

YeJin was receiving help and it looked as though she would be okay, eventually. But what about Sora? She was stronger than she thought she was and he knew she could get through this. A plan. He needed a plan.

He would need to nurse YeJin and they needed somewhere to hide, somewhere they could stay in one place while she recovered. Being on the run was not what he would recommend for people not trained in that activity, especially when they were weakened with a gun shot wound.

Would it be better to have Sora with them, so they could survive together? This was no kind of life for a young woman, but what was the alternative?

Then it came to him in a flash. Of course! Get her out of the country, to England. Clive would protect her and he couldn't think of anyone more qualified.

The NIS would be watching airports, so how could she get around them?

RaeWon didn't have any contacts in Seoul that could help. Would the old man have any? Could he ask him for more help? What about Clive? He had been in the same field as RaeWon, would he have any?

He dug in his pack for another phone that he had never used. In the pack was a sheet of paper which contained scribbled information from the past couple of days. In the corner was Clive's number. He dialed it.

The voice of Song EunJae came on the line.

"*Hello?*"

"Hello, this is Jung RaeWon, do you remember?"

"*Of course!*" She seemed happy to hear from him. "*How is Sora? We are looking forward to seeing her soon.*"

"Sora is well at the moment --"

He must have sounded less than positive and she pounced on it. "*What do you mean 'at the moment'? What is happening?*" She sounded more concerned now and RaeWon cursed himself for his lack of acting skills.

"I urgently need help from your husband. Is he available?" Back to business, his voice stronger.

Song EunJae was no stranger to people needing her husbands

help, but this was for a person lost for so many years and now found. "*What help do you need?*"

"It might be better if I spoke with him directly --"

"*How is your English. Let me translate. Tell me, what do you need?*"

RaeWon considered this for a moment. It seemed that she had done this before and wouldn't go to pieces. "I need air transport for Sora from Seoul to England. As soon as possible. But we have to presume that the NIS are watching the airports."

There was a short silence. "The NIS? *How bad is the situation?*"

"I think we are being framed for murder. We had a fire fight with the NIS and a friend was shot. Sora is alone somewhere in Seoul. Things could be better."

"*Can I call you back at this number?*"

"Yes."

"*Give me thirty minutes.*"

The call ended suddenly.

***

Sora woke to the sound of a dog barking in the distance. She looked at her phone and saw that she had been asleep for thirty minutes. The cardboard which had been covering her had fallen to the floor. She pulled it back over her and closed her eyes, but it didn't feel like sleep was going to come quickly this time. Still, she tried. The dog stopped barking and she started to doze.

***

Clive looked just as worried as he felt. "It doesn't look good."

"No," his wife agreed. "Perhaps Robert has an aircraft over there?"

Clive nodded. "I hope so. Let's ask."

He dialed a number.

"Robert, this is Clive and I need a favor. A big one."

"*Anything, just ask.*"

The two men had become firm friends after their sons had been involved in an aircraft crash in Afghanistan. Clive's son had rescued Robert's son from the wreckage and got the injured man to safety, avoiding enemy troops along the way. Robert felt a deep sense of gratitude for this act.

"Hear me out first before you volunteer. This will either be easy or not so easy."

"*Just tell me what you need.*"

"I have a young lady in Seoul who is being chased by the NIS. She is innocent of the charges, but she needs an urgent air lift out of the country. Do you have an aircraft in place that could help?"

"*Standby.*" The line went quiet and Clive could hear Robert using his computer keyboard. "*I do. It is actually a little south of Seoul and is preparing to depart soon. Straight line, it is about one hundred and ten clicks. Can she get that far?*"

"I doubt it, she has no trade craft and has survived on dumb luck so far."

There was a short pause. "*How important is this, Clive?*"

"I haven't seen this girl since she was born, but she is like a daughter to us."

"*Standby.*" Again Clive could hear the sounds of Robert on his keyboard and using another phone. "*Clive, get her to Seoul Air Base in Seongnam by 00:30 Seoul time. We will drop in and collect her.*"

"I don't want to risk an entire crew on this."

"*Why are they chasing her?*"

"They think she is an assassin."

"*I'll ask the crew. Bob is the load-master on this one, he can be very persuasive.*"

"How is he?"

"*Alive, thanks to your family. We can't bring her through the front door of the airfield, there is a lot of security for a Chinese government group. But I remember there is a service entrance on the southeast corner of the field. If she can get there, we will bring her in and load her. But ... she must get there quietly. If she is followed and someone sounds the alarm, we'll be flying through a lot of airspace that would not look kindly on her or the crew.*"

"Okay. She has help from a local asset who is also being hunted and he can tell her how to get there." Clive paused. "I don't know how to thank you, I'll explain everything later. But thank you."

"No problem, let me talk to Bob, but proceed as though the operation has a green light. Remember that if they won't let us land, the young lady will be on her own."

***

In the doctor's office, RaeWon made his way back to YeJin. As he entered the room, he found the woman tidying and picking up all the blood stained materials and instruments. The rags went in to a large bag and the instruments were readied for sterilization. When she was done, she washed her hands and stood drying them.

RaeWon looked at YeJin, who seemed peaceful.

The woman spoke first. "Your friend will recover completely, if you look after her during the next few weeks. The bullet went through and didn't damage anything on the way. I've cleaned and closed the wound. You will need to change the dressing periodically." She motioned to some bottles and supplies on the counter. "These are the medications and dressings you will need. This quantity should be sufficient."

RaeWon dug in his pack for money. "How much do I owe you? We really appreciate your help."

"There is no charge."

He hadn't expected this. She must have seen the look on his face.

"My father would be very angry if I took money from a friend."

"Your father?"

"Yes, the man you called for help." Another smile. "Ask him when you see him next. Your friend will sleep for another few hours. My colleague will return with a car in a few minutes. I won't ask where you are going, obviously, but I will wish you luck."

"Thank you ... both of you."

Noise from the entrance announced the return of her colleague. He appeared in the doorway, as cheerful as when he had left.

"The car is ready downstairs."

"Can we move her?" asked RaeWon.

"Oh yes. Just try to keep things a little quieter for her. My recommendation is that you find somewhere secluded to hide out for a couple of weeks. She certainly doesn't need to be on the road in this condition."

RaeWon nodded. "Of course."

"Contact me through my father if you need any help or advice while she recovers."

"Thank you." RaeWon shook her hand. "We should get moving."

CHAPTER EIGHTEEN

The Boeing 747 sat under the lights at Changju. There were a few less vehicles around her than ten minutes ago as the last of the small cargo was now being loaded.

Bob stood on the cargo deck monitoring the loading and checking that everything was secure. His phone rang.

"Dad! Everything okay? We're almost ready to depart."

He listened in silence to his father speak and then reached for his radio. "Stop fueling. Repeat, stop fueling." Back on the phone, "I understand, let me talk to the flight deck and get back to you."

He moved to the door and down the ladder on the K-loader to the ramp. He waved at the fueler who waved back. He raised his hands in an 'X' and the fueler gave him a thumbs-up. Satisfied that the fueling had been stopped, he climbed back on to the aircraft, up the stairs to the upper deck and on to the flight deck.

"Paul, I have a request from my father."

The captain laughed. "If he wants us to fill the aircraft with chocolate, I'm okay with that."

"No, it's a little more involved than that. He wants us to perform an extraction mission."

"I'm listening."

"A young lady needs a ride out of the country. She can get to Seoul Air Base. For an 00:30 exit if we can make it."

"We can try, but why do I feel this is more complicated?"

"She is being hunted by the NIS for something she didn't do."

Paul Hollingsworth took all of this in his stride. Since leaving the Royal Air Force he had missed some of the excitement. "How are we with the fuel and load? Will we be able to land there safely?"

I've stopped the fueling until I got your buy-in. The load is light, I just need to do the weight and balance to see what we can handle."

"Okay, you start on that and I'll brief the rest of the crew. I have an idea. Just make sure we are not overweight for the landing."

***

As promised, RaeWon's phone rang thirty minutes later. He raised it to his ear.

"This is RaeWon."

"Jung RaeWon-shi, this is Song EunJae. We have a possible solution. Do you have something to write on?"

"Yes." He scrambled for his pen. "Go ahead."

"Do you know the Seongnam air base?"

"Yes." He was surprised. That was not an airfield he would thought could have offered an escape. It was a military air base that also handled VIP flights for visiting heads of state.

"There is a cargo flight departing from Cheongju tonight. It will try to divert to Seongnam. The plan is to collect Sora and depart to Amsterdam. It will unload and take a new cargo, then fly to England. We will meet her on arrival. Can Sora get to Seongnam by 00:30?"

"I don't know her current location. But if she can, how will she get on to the base?"

"On the airfield perimeter there is a service entrance at the south-east corner. She will be met there and escorted to the aircraft. Does she have a passport with her?"

"Yes."

"*Good. Tell her that she must arrive quietly as there will be a lot of security for a Chinese government group. Arriving with people in pursuit will not work.*"

"Sora is better at this sort of thing than you might think. I have confidence in her."

"*Okay, then please give her the instructions and tell her we will see her soon.*"

"How did you find something so quickly?" RaeWon was incredulous that an escape option had been found with such speed.

"*We have good friends who are prepared to help when we ask. We can explain everything soon. This plan has a lot of risks but it is the best we could come up with at short notice. If they don't allow the aircraft to land, the plan is over. Let Sora know about the risks and please get her moving to the airfield.*"

"I hope I can repay you in the future."

"*Not necessary. Please look after your friend. We hope that we'll meet soon. Good bye.*"

RaeWon stared blankly at the wall, the phone hanging by his side. This plan was incredibly risky. Security would be all over the airfield. And what if they insisted on the aircraft landing somewhere else? Sora would be left unprotected again.

***

The phone vibrated in her pocket and Sora woke with a start, the noise seemed deafening, but in reality could not be heard more than a foot away. She was nervous.

"*Sora, are you awake?*"

"Yes."

"*Listen carefully, I need to give you some information. Are you ready, this is very important.*"

She rubbed her eyes with one hand as she spoke. "I'm ready."

"*Do you know Seongnam?*"

"No."

"*It is south east of the city, about twenty kilometers in a straight line. There is a military air base and I need you to go there.*"

"To a military base?" Sora was a little confused at the idea.

"*Yes. A civilian aircraft will be landing there at 00:30 to collect you ...*"

"But I can't just walk in," she interrupted.

"*I know,*" he said patiently, "*On the south east corner of the base is a service entrance. A man will meet you there, take you to the aircraft and fly you out of the country to Song EunJae. But, and this is very important, you must not be followed to the base. There will be a lot of security there and if you arrive running from people, the whole plan falls apart.*"

"I understand."

"*Also ...,*" he paused. "*A lot of other things could go wrong. The aircraft might not be allowed to land, or they might not be able to leave it to fetch you. So if you see the aircraft leave without you, you will need to keep running.*"

"Should we try to meet up if that happens?" she asked hopefully.

"*I don't know where we are going to be, Sora. I suggest you get out of town and lay low for a while, Then we can make contact and meet up.*"

"Okay. I can do that. Do you have any ideas for me to get to Seongnam?"

There was a pause and Sora heard the rustling of paper.

"*According to my map, there is a subway stop very close to that location. Let me check public transport.*"

"Will that be safe? I escaped on a motorbike, should I use that?"

"*No, get rid of the bike, preferably somewhere it won't be discovered too easily. You should be okay on a bus or subway as long as you avoid bus terminals. Those will be the easiest for them to monitor. And don't go anywhere near Gimpo or Incheon airports.*"

"Okay."

"*Where are you?*"

"I'm near Itaewon."

Another pause.

"*Plan A is for you to move to the road along the west side of Namsen Park. Take the 420 bus across the Han to Seolleong subway station. Take the train to Moran. Walk west and the airfield will be in front of you. Cross a river and the service entrance is right there. Approach carefully, very carefully. Got that?*"

Sora nodded as she finished making notes, even though she was on the phone. "Yes, I'll leave now. You said the plane arrives at 00:30? So I have over two hours."

"*Good luck. I really hope this works.*"

"I'll call you. Bye."

And then she was alone in the dark again. She checked the time: 21:45.

Sora had always been the type of person to arrive early. And her opinion had not changed with her small amount of field experience. She decided that it was better to be early and see what traps or problems lay in store.

She put her makeshift pillow back in the pack and hoisted it on her back. Taking a last look at her cardboard home, she waved and said goodbye. Sora emerged on to the narrow street and turned north, back toward Namsen Park. As she walked she realized that she was automatically keeping to the shadows. How would they be searching for her? She stopped. Or perhaps they didn't need to. The three of them had already provided enough evidence of their guilt. Sora was on camera as being at the building when the original shooting took place. Then they had fired on, and killed, some NIS agents. She shivered as she remembered that she had fired a gun at them herself. That was sure to be in their report. She started moving again. Perhaps they weren't looking at all, except perhaps in a very minor way. They couldn't know that she had photographs and video of the event, could they? She felt her pocket for the memory card. Still, best to assume the worst and expect traps everywhere.

Five minutes later she was climbing the steps at the side of the street where it rose sharply to join the road skirting the park. Just before leaving the steps, she took a look around for anyone waiting for her. She checked all the dark areas that would have been her first choice to ambush someone from. Nothing. Just to her right was the bus stop and she moved to a darkened area where she could stand and wait for the bus.

Six minutes later the bus arrived and she climbed aboard. As she sat down, it suddenly dawned on her that this was the start of her trip to safety. Toward the people in England who considered her family. It had been a while since there had been anyone in her life that was close and she couldn't help but wonder what that was like. As her head hit the window she realized she had nearly dozed off again. The bus was warm and it made her feel sleepy, but she forced herself to remain as alert as possible. You never knew who might get on at the next stop. She couldn't imagine how they could have agents boarding every bus in the city, but better to be prepared. She would sleep on the plane. If it arrived.

As the bus pulled away from the stop, a police car with lights flashing and siren blaring, approached rapidly from behind them and the bus slowed. At the last second the car turned off the road and down toward the hidden motorbike.

Sora was awake now.

CHAPTER NINETEEN

Ryu DaeHo was running out of ideas, out of his depth, or both.

The three suspects had evaded capture, killed and injured his men, were nowhere to be found, and had basically embarrassed him thoroughly. Of course, he spun this to his advantage, reporting that they were highly skilled and dangerous.

This worked to some degree with those who did not know the suspects, such as the local police. But for those within the NIS who knew both him and Jung RaeWon, it only served to solidify their opinion of Ryu DaeHo's abilities. And this was also the opinion of his bosses. Although they had selected him because they believed he would be easy to mold to their point-of-view, they also needed him to get results.

Ryu DaeHo was in a conference room with three subordinates.

"Our resources are limited, so how can we best use them to capture these three?" He looked around, hoping for a genius to present himself.

"Why are your resources so limited?" asked one of the men, idly stroking his cup of coffee.

"Yes," said another, "this is a little unusual."

Ryu DaeHo felt the meeting was going in the wrong direction.

"We're limited because of the status of the original operation. We have to keep a lid on this as much as possible. We can use local police, but other NIS assets are not available. So let's be positive and see what we can do rather than what we can't."

They all nodded and a quiet settled on the group.

The lone woman in the group spoke up. "Will they try to leave the country? Or stay domestic?"

The second man said, "Domestic."

"Why?"

"These are not hardened terrorists. Two of them are former NIS, and only one was a field agent. The third is new to us with no record at all. There are no known ties to foreign interests, no record of recent international travel; nothing that indicates overseas assets. Where would they go and how would they pay for it."

"Jung RaeWon was a field agent, he would have escape plans. That would be a matter of course for him."

'But he has been out of the NIS for a while. He may have got soft."

'They did shoot and kill several agents tonight," Ryu DaeHo reminded them. "I don't think any of them is soft."

"But I'm not even sure how they found out about the helicopter or what their goal was. Can we get more background?" said the first man.

"That is need-to-know only. Look, someone told them or they wouldn't have been waiting with a rifle," said Ryu DaeHo, re-writing history to his own ends. "I think we can assume that they were being paid to perform the kill and whoever is paying could be offering sanctuary."

The first man decided to speak up. "It seems very messy. One person on the roof and the other two rush in to rescue her? Something doesn't seem right."

A silence descended again.

Ryu DaeHo took the initiative. "We will have to stretch our capabilities. We'll assume that both domestic and international travel are a possibility. They might even split up. We will need to cover the airports, rail, and bus terminals. Obviously we can't cover every way of getting there, so we'll put static teams on site."

People were nodding in agreement.

"Pass their descriptions to local police and have them distribute the information to taxi, car rental companies, and hotels," he continued. "Any word from hospitals about a gunshot victim being treated?" Everyone shook their heads. "Keep monitoring that and let's get this information to the police now."

Everybody started gathering their papers and heading for the door. Soon Ryu DaeHo was left alone. He was very nervous about the way this mission was heading and he wasn't sure that he could bring it back on course.

***

The sound and lights of the police car quickly lessened as it disappeared down the road from which Sora had just emerged. The bus continued along the road and Sora pulled out her phone to get some idea of where she was going and how long the bus would take to get there. She stared at the screen. Forty minutes. Was this feeling of being trapped ever going to disappear, she wondered, or was it something that people on the run just got used to? She reminded herself that once she got to England everything would be okay, but would it? How could those people she had never met fix all her problems? On the other hand perhaps this aircraft that would take her away was sent by them?

She hadn't really thought about it, but how had RaeWon found a flight so quickly? And what kind of flight departed from a military airbase at midnight?

She had a lot of questions about what was about to happen. But no answers. Her uncle would have had the answers, he was that kind of man, she was sure. She remembered their last meeting in Hong Kong and regretted that she had not confided his identity to RaeWon and YeJin. She was alone again, at least until she reached England.

Sora was no stranger to her life being different than that of others around her and resolved that if this was her future, she would make the best of it. Although some people might have felt depressed at such a prospect, Sora was able to go with the flow and stubborn enough to think that she would get something positive from the experience.

As the bus passed over the river it made her feel better to imagine that all that water was between her and the scene of the crime. Just a little, not a lot.

As the journey progressed, people got on and people got off. The bus pushed its way through the traffic and Sora didn't see any more police cars or passengers who looked like they worked for the NIS. A couple of young guys got on and gave her a few glances, but as they did the same to other girls on the bus she decided not to worry about it.

The bus made a left turn and Sora knew she would need to get off soon. She checked the time; there was enough for her to be able to exercise some caution. One stop past the station, according to her phone, she got off and walked in to a store. She browsed for snacks, realizing how hungry she was. She took several chocolate bars and drinks. After she had paid, they were added to the camera equipment, radio, and gun in the backpack.

Was this normal stuff to carry around for the new person on the run, she thought? Probably so.

At the store entrance, she carefully looked around for the usual suspicious people and confident there was no one that meant to do her harm, she stepped outside and started walking back toward the subway station entrance.

Then she felt a hand on her shoulder.

CHAPTER TWENTY

The vehicle that RaeWon was taken to in the parking area was a minivan. It was the best choice. The sliding door allowed them easy access to get YeJin inside. They sat YeJin in a rear seat and reclined it as far as it would go. There was even a box provided to raise her feet. They fastened the seatbelt and stood back to admire their handiwork.

Presumably they had chosen the same type of vehicle before, but RaeWon had to admit that it seemed as though they had scoured every dealership in the city to find the perfect transportation.

As he went to close the door, he saw some bags. He turned to ask about them, but his helper simply shrugged his shoulders and smiled shyly.

"I thought if you were going to a hiding place you might not want to stop and buy groceries, so we got some for you."

"Perfect!" said RaeWon, shaking his hand. "Thank you."

As he drove the vehicle out of the garage he continued to be careful about the cars around them. Was anyone following? Unlikely, he thought, but it never hurt to be careful.

Should he meet Sora so they could all stay together? Was he unintentionally using her as bait to lure the NIS after her as she made her away across Seoul? No, it was better for her to take the chance of getting to England. If she stayed in Korea they would continue to pursue her. And if they all stayed together, it would increase the chance of them all being caught. Much better to let her run.

Another thoughtful touch was the map book which had been left on the seat. He knew where he was going, but what would be the best way to get there? As usual it was best to assume the worst and plan accordingly.

On the other hand, sometimes it just paid to not over-think things. Decision made, he headed east on Olympic, following the south bank of the Han. Traffic was flowing smoothly and he made good time through the darkness. As they drove past bridges over the river leading to the north bank, he saw police cars checking cars on two of them. He did not intend to cross to the north, but would have to use one bridge soon.

The van hummed along steadily. RaeWon took bites from an apple as he drove, his tension rising slightly as knew they were approaching the last bridge, where Olympic became the Gyeongchun Expressway. As they got closer, he saw the lights of a police car. The traffic slowed. As he got nearer, he could see vehicles being waved to the side of the road. The he realized that this was a random traffic stop. Perhaps it wasn't even part of the hunt for the three of them.

RaeWon checked the gun on the seat next to him and moved it a little closer. He certainly didn't want to kill anyone else tonight, so he tried to think positively as they slowed even more.

The red car in front of him was waved over and the policeman started to wave him over too. Then another policeman called out that they had enough for the moment and the officer in front of RaeWon waved him on down the road.

Past the road block, the very light traffic started to pick up speed and he started to enjoy the apple again.

Though he was familiar with his destination, he was not so sure about this particular road and he watched carefully for his exit. The road passed through several tunnels and the road noise coupled with his tiredness made him aware of how much he was looking forward to and needed some sleep.

Twenty minutes later he saw the sign for the exit and he pulled off the Expressway, negotiated some junctions and headed north, a little more slowly on the much smaller road.

He picked a dark spot where he could safely park off the road, pulled over and turned off the lights. He looked back at YeJin who continued to sleep. He smiled as he thought of her reaction to him thinking about how pretty she was despite the dark. She was sure to have some sarcastic comment about how a lack of light always made her look better.

Picking up his phone, he dialed a number.

"This is Jung RaeWon - - Yes, I'm well - - I need some help. Can I use the guest house on your farm? - - Thank you, I will be there in about forty minutes. I'll give you the story when I get there and if I can still stay - - Wait until you have all the facts. I'll be there soon - - Yes, bye."

It was one thing to ask an asset in a foreign country for help, especially if they could move when things got too hot, but it was quite another to ask friends to help when they weren't in the business and might not fully understand what they were exposing themselves to.

He drove on uneventfully through the night, the headlights picking out things that reminded him what the countryside looked like.

Before he reached the outskirts of the village, he turned off the road through an open gate and stopped in front of a low house with it's blue roof. The gate was closed behind him, enclosing the van within the six foot high wall. A small man moved awkwardly toward the van, his back bent slightly as he walked. He knocked on the window and motioned toward the open door of the barn. RaeWon nodded and parked the van inside, turning off the engine and enjoying the silence that followed.

He got out and leaving YeJin he walked to the man. They embraced warmly.

"It's been a long time," said the man with reproach.

"It has," agreed RaeWon. "But let me tell you what's going on ..."

"Aren't you going to get your friend out of the car?"

"There is still nothing wrong with your eyes, I see. If we're going to move her we should do it once."

"A woman? Are things so bad that you had to drug a woman to get her to follow you?"

"No, she has been shot."

The man grabbed him by the arm. "Then bring her inside. Now."

"But let me explain before you agree --"

"Fool! I don't care what the problem is, bring her inside!"

RaeWon carried YeJin and followed the man in to his home. Inside, the man led the way to a bedroom where he laid several blankets on the floor to make a more comfortable space for YeJin. RaeWon laid her down and the man inspected the bandaged area.

"It was treated well," he allowed. Without looking up, he added, "What kind of trouble are you in?"

RaeWon sighed. And started to explain.

***

Sora felt the hand on her shoulder and instantly blamed herself for being too complacent. Why had she ever thought that she could evade the authorities and escape out of the country. Was she crazy?

At the same time, her fight instinct kicked in. If she had not been on a busy street she would have taken the wrist attached to the hand and broken the arm attached to the wrist. But, she reminded herself, she needed to get to the airfield without a tail and running away was not helpful.

So, she turned slowly and put a puzzled expression on her face. Standing behind her was a policeman, not much older than herself. She knew his age because she knew the man in the uniform. Or she thought she had known him at one point recently. Now, however, despite the fact that there were a lot of people she did not want to see, he was the absolute last person on the planet that she was willing to tolerate spending even one second with.

But people were watching, so she restrained her desire for violence in this case and took a half step back.

He held up both hands to indicate that he meant no harm. Sora looked around for his partner but couldn't see anyone. They stood in silence for a moment, a long moment, and she didn't think that she was doing a good job of hiding her distaste from him.

"Sora, I'm glad to see you are well. I've missed you since you left."

"You didn't give me much choice about staying or leaving," she said.

He looked embarrassed. As he should.

"I wanted to apologize." He looked around. "Seeing as how you are a wanted person, can we at least get off the street for a moment. We're probably on camera at the moment and I may need to explain how you got away."

Sora controlled her expression a little better this time. So he knew that she was wanted. She had no reason to trust him, but he did seem a little more like the person she had once known.

"Let's get a drink," she said.

He nodded and led the way to a nearby cafe.

She sat at a table and waited for him to return with the drinks. As he sat, he spoke on his radio. "Hyung, I've met a friend. I'll be taking a break."

Sora crinkled her face at being described as his friend. But it was better than fugitive.

He sat opposite and the air between them was very awkward.

"I'm sorry," he said "I don't know what came over me --"

"Soju," she interrupted.

"Yes." He stopped. "I'm sorry."

Another awkward silence.

"I don't believe you did what they said you did," he continued.

"What do they say that I did?"

"That you assassinated a government employee, killed an NIS officer, and tried to kill others while making your escape --"

"I didn't kill anyone, but I did shoot at some people who were shooting at me. It was self defense." She hadn't touched the drink yet.

He took a sip from his drink. It was hot and he almost burnt himself.

"You shot at people? You had a gun? This doesn't sound like you."

"People will do the funniest things when they have to."

"But you were so sweet and innocent --"

"Was that why you and your friends tried to rape me?"

He slowly put the drink down. "I'm very sorry. It was the alcohol. I haven't touched any since then. I was so worried after you left. I'm just glad to see that you're okay."

"Physically, I'm fine. But when your boyfriend and two of his friends try to do something like that, it changes you. And when the NIS try to pin a crime on you ... Well, yes, I've changed a little. But I'm okay, I guess."

It had been the first time that she had used her fighting skills in a real situation. It had felt good to leave the three of them lying on the floor. She had left his apartment, gone home and packed, and moved out that same day. In the six months since it happened she had done her best to forget it. But she had to admit that channeling those same feelings when she had saved YeJin had felt good, too. But this guy was still scum to her.

Was he going to arrest her? It didn't seem so.

"What happens now?" she asked. She didn't want to come out and say it, but she was going to fight her way out of this if she had to.

"Nothing. I don't believe you are the international terrorist they seem to be saying you are. Don't tell me where you are going just in case they ask me."

She still hadn't touched the drink.

"So I'm free to go?"

"Yes."

Neither of them moved, the drinks sat on the table between them.

"Sora, I'm really, really sorry about what happened."

The new Sora started to feel the slightest bit sorry for the old boyfriend, but she stopped the feeling as soon as she recognized it.

"I'm leaving," she said. She looked at a clock on the wall. "I have a bus to catch. I think I need some mountain air."

She stood, put the pack on her back, and walked out. She watched his reflection in the glass window. He didn't move. Once outside, she crossed the street and headed south. She would walk to the next subway station down the line. If they searched the CCTV at Seollang, she didn't want to be on it. And she knew from her phone that the next station was only a kilometer to the south.

She started walking.

***

The train pulled in to the Moran subway station, gradually slowing to a stop. The doors opened and Sora grasped the backpack, joining the knot of people leaving the train. On the platform she stayed with the group, doing her best to look like just another traveler, even pretending to be part of a conversation so as not to appear to be on her own.

She followed her new friends to the surface and didn't see anyone suspicious on the way. Remembering how complacent she had been before getting on to the train, she was being extra careful. This was the last stretch of her journey, in Seoul anyway, and she didn't want to collect a tail at this important time.

Above ground, she left her group and pausing for a moment to get her bearings with the help of her phone, set off toward the airfield to the west.

As she walked through the darkness, she forced herself to pay attention to her surroundings and not hurry too much. She had plenty of time to make her flight and she smiled at thinking of her escape this way. She didn't know exactly what was going to happen at the airfield, but was sure it was guaranteed to be different from the times she had traveled on an airline before.

Ahead, the road she was on ended at an intersection where a road crossed from north to south. She stood at the side of the road and waited to cross. As she looked at the other side it was unlit between her and the wall that surrounded the air base. She had expected men with guns guarding the field, but all she could see was the wall and the glow of lights on the other side. An aircraft noisily descended from her left and disappeared behind the wall.

She crossed the road and on the other side found a smaller road leading to a narrow bridge, just wide enough for a car, which spanned a small river. Before crossing the bridge, Sora stopped and carefully checked what she could see ahead. Slowly she was able to see that across the water, the road turned to the left and followed the river and airfield wall. No people were visible and no vehicles were moving. There was a small parking area on this side of the water where people parked to use the jogging track which she could see below her. But no one was exercising.

Sora checked the time: 23:40. Her flight would arrive soon. She crossed the river, followed the road as it turned, and looked at the wall as she walked south. Somewhere was a way through the wall and she wanted to locate it before looking for somewhere to hide out of sight until someone appeared to take her to the aircraft.

A few minutes later she reached a part of the wall where there had once been a gate large enough to drive vehicles through. But not anymore. At some time the gate had been replaced with a new piece of wall. They had, however, installed a door in the wall for people to move through. It looked very solid and she wasn't sure how they intended to open it unless they had a key. Surely people don't make access too easy at military bases?

She didn't pause as she passed the door, but kept moving and looked for somewhere to wait. A minute later she was standing next to another parking area. There was only one car sitting there, but there were a few small trees. She selected a tree and sat with her back against it. She had a good view of the doorway and clutching the pack to her chest she tried her best to make herself a part of the tree.

CHAPTER TWENTY-ONE

The aircraft was still sitting under the lights at Cheongju.

The swarm of service vehicles had been moved away from her body and Bob was double checking his calculations. Everything looked fine; they had enough fuel to get across Russian air space, although they might have to stop at Helsinki to refuel if the winds were not as advertised, and they would be just below maximum landing weight at Seongnam.

The crew were assembled on the flight deck and Paul was turned in his seat to address them. "Does everyone understand the plan?"

Everyone nodded.

"Anyone not want to do this? Speak up, now is the time to say something."

Everyone remained silent as he moved his eyes between the other three men.

"Okay, then let's make this happen."

There was a flurry of activity as the engineer triple checked his instruments and they all adjusted their seats and fastened their harnesses. The co-pilot had the charts for Seongnam ready.

Paul keyed his microphone to talk to the people on the ramp.

"Ground, Flight Deck, we are ready to push."

"Release brakes."

"Brakes are released."

"Starting push-back."

After a moment the aircraft began to move slowly rear-wards and away from the warehouses which held the cargo they had delivered the previous day. Two minutes later, the last piece of ground equipment was disconnected and they started the engines, one by one.

"Cheongju Ground, Albatross one zero three heavy is ready to taxi."

"Albatross one zero three heavy taxi to runway zero six left."

Paul acknowledged the instructions and applied power to begin their short journey to the runway. The large aircraft gently moved forward and the crew continued their pre-takeoff checks. Soon the alternating lights ahead of them announced the runway and the aircraft came to a stop.

"Cheongju Tower, Albatross one zero three heavy is ready for takeoff, zero six left."

The tower approved their request and they moved forward again on to the runway, turning until the concrete and lights stretched ahead of them. Paul moved the throttles forward and they watched the instruments to make sure the engines were spooling together. Satisfied, a final movement made them move forward, slowly at first but gradually increasing speed.

The first officer called out the speeds and Paul rotated the aircraft toward the sky. The landing gear was raised and the flaps retracted, the aircraft gaining more speed as it climbed toward the north west and Seoul.

They flew in silence for a few minutes, altering course slightly to the north to stay on their path.

The first officer broke the heavy silence. "We just passed Suwon Air Base. Time to start the plan."

Suwon was a little over half-way to Seoul.

"Seoul Center, Albatross one zero three heavy."

"Go ahead."

"Seoul, we are experiencing a problem with a warning indicator on our number three engine and would like to enter a hold at Anyang while we investigate."

The request was approved and they followed instructions to descend. Soon they were flying a race-track pattern.

"Everyone know the plan?" said Paul. "Pickup time is between 00:30 and 01:00, so if we hold for another ten minutes, we should arrive there right on time. Bob, are you ready?"

"Yes, sir."

"Okay then." He turned to the flight engineer. "How is our weight looking for the landing?"

"It's looking good."

Silence returned to the flightdeck as they continued to fly their holding pattern. Ten minutes later, he called the controller again.

"Seoul Center, Albatross one zero three heavy."

"*Go ahead.*"

"Albatross one zero three heavy is requesting diversion to Seoul Air Base."

"*Standby.*" There was a pause and they could all picture the controller coordinating the request with Seongnam. "*Albatross one zero three heavy, their ramp is closed due to VIP traffic, can you accept an alternate?*"

"Seoul, ramp space not required. We think we know what the problem is and we will only need to be on the ground for a few minutes. No ground support is required."

There was another pause and everyone on-board the freighter held their breath.

"*Albatross one zero three heavy, request approved. Turn right heading zero nine zero. Contact Seoul Approach one two three decimal eight.*"

Paul acknowledged the instructions as he turned the aircraft toward Seongnam. "That was easier than I expected, I hope it's a good omen."

***

As they descended through six thousand feet, the lights of Seoul filling the view to the north, Paul retarded the throttles a little more.

"We're going to be on the ground soon," he said. "Everyone

ready for this?"

This wasn't the first time he had asked the crew, but not all of them had military experience and he wanted to make sure they had thought about what they were about to do. At best they would make it out of Seoul with no one suspecting what they had done. At worst someone would find out and they would be intercepted in Chinese or Russian air space on their way back to Europe. Everybody nodded but didn't say anything.

"Albatross one zero three heavy, report established on the ILS for runway zero two."

Paul acknowledged the instruction and began a gradual left turn to intercept the landing system.

A few minutes later the airfield lights were visible ahead of them.

"One thousand feet," the co-pilot called out. "Five hundred."

Paul brought the throttles back and concentrated on his landing spot. He gently flared the aircraft and they barely felt the main gear begin rolling on the concrete behind them. The spoilers deployed, destroying the lift created by the wing.

"Reverse thrust."

The co-pilot pulled the throttles all the way back and past the detent and into the reverse position. They pictured the engines now pushing forward instead of back and felt the aircraft lose speed as they headed down the runway.

"Ninety knots," said the co-pilot and moved the throttles to idle.

Paul maintained his braking.

"Sixty knots."

"Tower, one zero three requesting backtrack on runway one nine. We think we have the problem fixed and just need a couple of minutes at the hold before we're ready to depart."

"Approved."

Bob said what they were all thinking. "Is this too easy?"

Nobody answered him.

CHAPTER TWENTY-TWO

June 04

At 00:30, Sora started paying more attention to landing aircraft. After a few minutes a bright light appeared to the south. As it got closer it dissolved in to several lights. This was a large aircraft and she thought that the wheels hanging below it really did make it look like a bird ready to grab on to a wire and rest.

Was this her way out? Surely it would be something smaller. How many people would something like that carry? A lot, she was sure. A picture came to mind of her walking on to the aircraft and hundreds of people looking to see who had interrupted their journey.

Regardless of any future embarrassment, it was time for her contact to appear. Putting the pack on her back she moved closer to the rendezvous point and waited.

***

When they had slowed to a crawl and the end of the runway was in sight, Paul swung the aircraft nose to the left and then turned the beast to the right to head down the adjacent runway.

This was their ideal scenario. Once they got to the south end of the runway they would be very close to the perimeter wall that was between them and their passenger.

"One zero three, hold at the south end of the runway and advise if you require assistance."

"One zero three," acknowledged the co-pilot.

They continued slowly south, with Bob craning to see the wall out of the window.

"Cargo ties?" suggested Paul.

Bob agreed and disappeared to gather a couple of the straps used to secure cargo. Straps over his shoulder, he took a hand-held radio that they used to communicate on the ground amongst the crew, and descended to the main deck where he located the panel in the floor that gave access to the aircraft radios and electronics below. With the panel open, he dropped the straps in to the darkness and followed them down using the ladder attached to the wall. At the bottom of the ladder he moved to the center of the aircraft and stood next to a hatch in the floor. He clipped the radio to his belt and put the ear-piece in his left ear.

"Paul, this is Bob. I'm ready."

"Standby. Thirty seconds. Be careful."

Steadying himself against the rack of equipment, he waited.

He felt the aircraft slowing to a stop and then felt the lack of forward motion.

"Bob. Go, go, go."

"On my way." He knelt and opened the hatch. Below him he saw the concrete of Seoungnam. As the aircraft taxi lights were extinguished, he pushed the straps out and lowered the ladder, then climbed down, dropping the last few feet to the ground. The aircraft was facing to the south and he saw the wall to his left. Where was the door? He scooped the straps over his shoulder again and moved toward the wall. At the wall he decided to move to his right. He followed the wall and it didn't take long to see where the material changed and had replaced the old gate. He saw the door.

Try the obvious first, he told himself. He looked for a handle and any devices that might signal his presence to the authorities.

He didn't see any electronics, but he did see a large chain and padlocks securing the door. He would have to use the straps.

The wall was about ten feet tall and the straps were twelve feet long. He fastened the ends of two straps together. Coiling one end, he started to windmill his arm to put some force behind the throw and lofted the strap over the wall.

***

Sora watched as the aircraft she had seen land disappeared behind the wall and away from her. Two minutes later she heard a noise getting louder and saw the top of the aircraft reappear, this time toward her. It stopped, facing in her direction. This had to be for her, she thought. Another two minutes and an object appeared over the top of the wall. What was it? A rope?

She ran toward it and saw that it was a large metal fastener at the end of a red strap. It was unlikely that it was standard practice for people to throw this kind of thing over a wall in the middle of the night, so she grabbed it and pulled. Twice.

Someone pulled twice from the other side. She removed her backpack and tied it to the end of the strap, then grabbed the strap and started to climb. The wall was rough which provided enough traction for her feet to help her ascend.

At the top she lay on her stomach and looked down the other side. The aircraft sat looking at her, it's landing lights turned off. It looked so good, so friendly to her. Like a giant, protecting animal. She didn't know what kind it was, but it was instantly her favorite aircraft of all time.

A man was waiting below her. It was hard to tell in the dark, but he didn't seem to be Korean. He said something which she could not hear above the aircraft noise. He beckoned to her. Definitely not Korean. She pulled the strap up from where she had just climbed and lowered the backpack inside the wall. She thought the wall looked about ten feet high. She rolled off the wall, landed on the ground and rolled to absorb the impact.

She felt the man helping her to her feet. He gathered the strap and looked around for any evidence that they had been there. He faced Sora and pointed to the aircraft. She nodded and they ran toward the front of the aircraft. Sora had no idea how you got on to an aircraft when it was already on the runway with its engines running, but apparently this wasn't going to be a problem for the man next to her.

The noise was loud, but welcoming and seemed to help hide them, at least in her mind.

They passed under the nose and she saw a ladder hanging from a hole in the bottom of the aircraft. The man took her arm and pointed upward. She nodded, handed him her backpack, and climbed the six feet into the bottom of the aircraft. She reached back down and took the straps and then the backpack from the man. He followed her up the ladder and in to the cramped space. He pulled the ladder inside and closed the hatch. Reaching for a radio, he said something in to it. A moment later Sora felt and heard the engine noise increase and the beast started to gently turn. The man pointed to the ladder on the wall and they both climbed out. Sora was surprised by the almost empty, cavernous interior. No need to be worried about being embarrassed in front of passengers, she thought. He replaced the floor panel and led her the short distance to another ladder, leading to the upper deck, which they both climbed. The aircraft continued it's slow turn.

Upstairs, Sora took a seat and fastened her seat belt, backpack on the seat next to her. She leaned back, looked out of the window and breathed for what seemed like the first time in hours.

***

Bob made sure the girl was seated and headed on to the flight-deck. Out of the windows he could see that they had turned one hundred and eighty degrees and were now facing north.

Paul keyed the radio. "Tower, Albatross one zero three heavy is ready for departure. Requesting runway zero two."

"One zero three, taxi to runway zero two, position and hold."

Paul applied breakaway power and they slowly started moving

towards the taxiway linking the two runways. Everyone was quiet, afraid of letting all the people on the ground know what they had done. But everything seemed normal. At the runway they positioned the aircraft to use every available meter of concrete and came to a stop.

They waited while several helicopters departed to the east and then the tower cleared them for take-off.

Paul moved the throttles forward, the flight engineer watching the dials to make sure all the engines were responding. Paul released the brakes and she moved forward with a definite purpose in mind; next stop Europe. The nose lifted in to the air. Wheels and flaps retracted, they followed instructions and began a climb over Seoul and turned towards Incheon, on their way westward.

He handed over control to the co-pilot and turned to Bob.

"Good work. Is she okay? How did she seem?"

Bob shrugged. "I got the impression from my father that she is just a civilian. But I have to say, she was very calm and in control of herself. Most people would have freaked out at being hauled over a wall on to a military base and then having to climb in to a large, noisy aircraft. But not this one."

"I'm curious about the story, if its not classified. Does she speak English?"

"Haven't had a chance to find out yet." He looked back though the open door to the upper-deck area. "She seems to be asleep. Must have had a busy day."

***

At around the same time that Sora was drifting off to sleep, YeJin was waking at the farm. She stirred on the blankets and RaeWon leaned over and dabbed her forehead with a damp cloth. Her eyes flickered open, closed, and then gradually opened again.

"Welcome back," he said. "You're going to be okay. Not today or tomorrow, but soon."

She made a face as she felt the effects of the bullet that had gone through her body.

"You were shot," he reminded her. "I got you to a doctor and she patched you up. There is going to be some pain for a few days."

He put a glass of water to her lips and she turned her head to take a sip.

"Where are we?" she asked.

"Somewhere they won't find us."

"Sora?"

"On her way to England."

She was quiet for a moment and then glanced around. "Do you bring all your girls here?"

"Only when they've been shot."

She smiled and went back to sleep. RaeWon picked up his gun, checked the magazine and satisfied, put the gun on a small table at his side. He was tired and made himself as comfortable as he could. He was sure that YeJin would have something to say about it when she woke, but he was going to stay right next to her.

EPILOGUE

June 05 | 21:00
Hong Kong International Airport

Kim JiMin was the only person not moving on the rail station at Hong Kong airport. She had just arrived from the city and her fellow travelers were swarming around her on the way to their flights. She stood, phone to her ear, one bag over her shoulder and another pulled behind her.

The voice on the phone seemed stressed.

"The mission is confirmed, you are cleared for travel. Operation parameters remain as discussed. Do you have any questions?" said Ryu DaeHo.

"I have a lot of questions about your groups' management of this operation so far --"

"Do you have any questions regarding phase two?" he interrupted.

"What happened to the fugitives, the ex-agents and the girl?"

"They have gone to ground and are no longer a threat. The first phase was a success and you are cleared for phase two."

"So you don't know where they are or why they were involved? This sounds like a loose end."

"The police have been alerted to their identities and are looking for them. The girl was in the wrong place at the wrong time. It was coincidence. They

can not possibly have any knowledge about the operation."

"You had better be right --"

"And you had better perform as we need you to. Remember what is at stake for you."

She did remember. "I will complete the contract."

"This is the last target and then you are finished."

Perhaps not, she thought to herself as she ended the call, she might make an exception and perform one more job.

Checking the time she hurried to her flight.

***

Waiting at the gate to board her flight she wondered, not for the first time, if this really was the end. It was her last contract, she knew that. Having been forced to take this job by the NIS she was determined to finish it as quickly as possible and return to the life she wanted.

Ryu DaeHo was not as concerned about the three that had escaped as she was. But he did not know everything that she knew.

They did have some knowledge. They knew what she looked like, knew that she was the shooter, and may even have photographic evidence. From her point of view this was a problem. A big one.

Of course there were people that knew what she looked like and some of them even knew what she did for a living. But there were very few and all of them were on her side of the fence; unlikely to disclose that information.

She really, really wanted to be back in Korea searching for these three people.

Was it enough that they had to keep their heads down while the entire Korean police force was looking for them?

What was to stop them releasing the camera footage to prove their innocence? Not that they were really innocent, they had killed federal agents. If the police did find them, they might be beaten to a pulp or simply shot before they could say anything in their own defense.

She hadn't told the NIS about the camera for one important reason: two lives would be in danger. Her own, because the NIS would throw her to the wolves and she would become one of the loose ends that she was being paid to tidy up. And her sister, who until a few months ago had been hidden away at university.

She really was in the middle, between the fugitives and the NIS, both having information about her that they should not have. Perhaps after this trip her last mission should be to remove one side of this equation?

An announcement interrupted her thoughts.

"Ladies and gentlemen, flight zero two six to London is ready for boarding ..."

Thank you for reading this book!

If you would like to stay up-to-date with this series, please visit:

www.AndrewDThompsonBooks.com

and consider subscribing to our email list.